A
PARCEL OF
THEIR FORTUNES

Written by Barbara Ninde Byfield

A PARCEL OF THEIR FORTUNES
A HARDER THING THAN TRIUMPH
FOREVER WILT THOU DIE
SOLEMN HIGH MURDER (WITH FRANK L. TEDESCHI)

SMEDLEY HOOVER: HIS DAY (WITH SARA KRULWICH)
THE BOOK OF WEIRD (ORIGINAL TITLE: THE GLASS
   HARMONICA)
THE EATING IN BED COOKBOOK

ANDREW AND THE ALCHEMIST
THE HAUNTED TOWER
THE HAUNTED GHOST
THE HAUNTED CHURCHBELL
THE HAUNTED SPY

Illustrated by Barbara Ninde Byfield

TALES OF TERROR AND MYSTERY BY SIR ARTHUR CONAN DOYLE
HADASSAH: ESTHER THE ORPHAN QUEEN BY WILLIAM H.
   ARMSTRONG
THE CABLE CAR AND THE DRAGON BY HERB CAEN
TV THOMPSON BY GLENDON AND KATHRYN SWARTHOUT
THE MYSTERY OF THE SPANISH SILVER MINE BY HARVEY
   SWADOS
THE GIANT SANDWICH BY SETH M. AGNEW
UPRIGHT HILDA BY DONALD HUTTER

A
PARCEL OF
THEIR FORTUNES

BARBARA NINDE BYFIELD

PUBLISHED FOR THE CRIME CLUB BY

DOUBLEDAY & COMPANY, INC.

GARDEN CITY, NEW YORK

1979

All of the characters in this book are fictitious,
and any resemblance to actual persons,
living or dead, is purely coincidental.

41528

Library of Congress Cataloging in Publication Data

Byfield, Barbara Ninde.
A parcel of their fortunes.

I. Title.
PZ4.B9936Par [PS3552.Y65]   813'.5'4
ISBN: 0-385-14611-6
Library of Congress Catalog Card Number 79-7565

For
Libby and George Alsberg
who helped me to go

and for
Kinza and Philip Schuyler
who made it possible to stay

. . . Men's judgements are
A parcel of their fortunes, and things outward
Do draw the inward quality after them,
To suffer all alike.

—*Antony & Cleopatra* III xiii 31

A
PARCEL OF
THEIR FORTUNES

Prologue CRUMBLES

It was an utterly middle-aged day from the beginning. Helen stood at the kitchen window watching Mr. Penner's truck following his own white Daimler as they ground up the driveway, skirting the more avoidable lakes of mud. She wondered what arcane knowledge the builder had, to be sure it would not rain today and so to bring his men to work on the roof at last. The sky was the same color of dead bluefish as it had been for the last eight days; the absence of actual sheets of rain was hardly noticeable. However, she was no authority on the weather of Kent nor of any other part of England; if Penner thought today was the day for mending the leaking thatch that covered the original two rooms of the old house, so much the better. The plaster ceiling of the one bedroom beneath it was pendulous with damp. And the roof was the last of the things Simon had contracted with Penner to do; Helen would be rather glad to see the last of him.

She tied a piece of clothesline around an old cassock of Simon's she was using as a bathrobe and put the kettle on the stove. Noticing glumly that in five more days she could tear grease-spotted November off the calendar, she wondered if December could be any worse. Snow might be decorative for a day or two; the sheets of standing water and the quagmire that now stood where the old chicken house had been might even freeze and look attractive for a bit. At least the truckload of rotten shingles and rusted chicken wire had been carted off before Simon had left; he'd been full of plans for a small sunken pond and garden just there, with the old willow as background. Iris, he'd said, and azaleas; water hyacinth but no goldfish. Definitely no goldfish. "I didn't get rid of my son's chickens at long last just to take on another tyranny of mouths to feed." Helen smiled; she was privately of the opinion that Fergus would be, if anything, more pleased than his father to be free of the last three of that sickly brood. An enthusiasm taken on at sixteen was not necessarily meant to last even a decade. Fergus was, in any event, turning into as peripatetic a landlord as his father; his young film production company now needed the presence and attention he'd once given to those miserable birds.

"Good morning, Mr. Penner." She stepped out the kitchen door, her feet in heavy rubber boots, onto the tiny stone doorstep. "Um, those little plants just there along the wall—they look like twigs, I know, but could your guys be a little careful? They're some climbing hydrangeas we've just put in."

"Here now, here now, Alf, Ralph, mind Father Bede's flowers along there." The two young men who were flinging ladders, hooks, blocks, tackle, and piles of fresh thatch from the truck looked askance at Helen's garb and the pathetic sticks of what Simon hoped would be magnificent green covering the north wall one day. She'd twitted him that what he really wanted was Instant Versailles, especially after the nursery man had advised him that these didn't "do much" for the first five years.

"Simon back yet, Helen?" Penner advanced carefully up the slippery stepping-stone walk, unbuttoning his black ponyskin coat which glistened almost as much as his patent leather loafers. "Here you are, brought up the things from the postbox for you, save you a trip. Need a few loads of gravel on that drive, you do."

"Yes, we do. Thanks for the mail. No, Simon's still

away—yes, please, do come in." She followed him into the kitchen, both of them trailing fresh mud to add to the crazed old linoleum. Penner was disapprovingly aware of her garb, her uncombed hair, the wooden sink piled with lazy dishes from three scratch meals. She wished she had a dead canary in an uncleaned cage to top it all off. Mrs. Penner, she was sure, was, with one hand, now putting the last fine touches on a steak-and-kidney pie and tucking it into a surgically clean oven, while with the other ironing her husband's shirts to perfection. Or, more likely, maids were attending to that while Mrs. Penner motored into London in her Rover to have her diamonds cleaned.

"I had another telegram yesterday, he's gotten sucked into something else now for at least a week—yes, do sit down." She laid Simon's mail—a letter with a foreign stamp from Fergus, a bill from the nursery man, the *Times*, something from Lambeth—beside him on the rickety table by the rumpsprung armchair where Penner, feet up, was lighting a cigar.

"Pity. Last chance to persuade him into tearing this little bit of thatch off altogether and doing a proper tile job like the rest of the house. Sure he's set on thatch?"

"Yes, I'm sure. Both he and Fergus are fond of it—how clever of you, the fire does need some coal, thanks." Penner had leaned forward and dumped the remainder of the scuttle of coal onto the red embers in the little iron grate. "Perhaps another year, too, when they haven't laid out quite so much on other things, but he told me specifically just to have the bad patch over the bedroom done now. Oh dear—!" Crashings of ominous heaviness came from above; she saw a sheaf of ancient thatch flung down outside the window, followed by another. "They won't do more than they have to, will they? I know Simon's concerned about the expense, he's done so much already."

"Penny wise, pound foolish. If you're going to stir the pot, stir it from the bottom, says I."

"Yes, well, just the bad bit over the bedroom for now. And please do have a look at the paper while I get dressed." She left the builder deep in the financial section of the *Times* and closed the door into the bedroom, propping it shut with a chair since the jamb was swollen with damp.

Was it wiser to make the bed now and hope some millionth of a BTU left from her body warmth would remain during the day, or leave it unmade and hope some of the damp deep within the mattress would evaporate? Either way, it felt every night like getting in between two slices of bologna, the sheets and blankets were so sad and chill. Leave it unmade. She pulled on her thermal underwear, corduroy pants and old black sweater, tossing the cassock and her flannel nightshirt on the chair. The closet in this room had a distinct leak of its own; the bucket underneath it undoubtedly needed emptying.

Sticking her tongue out at the week's letters and telegrams from Simon that lay on the packing crates Fergus had improvised long ago for a dresser, she glared at herself in the greenish mirror hanging from a string against the pocked and peeling wallpaper. Be fair, she told herself, you're only cross with him because he's off doing something that sounds like fun and you're not along. She leaned closer to the mirror—maybe I really *am* that ghastly looking. If so, how could he possibly have taken her along to the late Anthea's family gathering, someone with wrinkles and acne at the same time—that really is a thing coming out on my chin, damnit—who needs a haircut and hasn't a stitch to her name that's presentable. To say nothing of my hands; sandpaper burns and walnut varnish stain aren't "in" this year.

Almost morbidly she picked up the photograph of Fergus's mother, Anthea, that he kept on the dresser.

Fair, fine-boned, if she'd lived she'd be almost fifty now, Helen thought, like me, but still with lovely translucent skin, no freckles; *she* would have worn garden hats and driven in gloves. Driven. She'd been killed in an automobile crash when Fergus was fifteen. Simon had bought this silly weekend place shortly afterward, keeping his son and himself busy and together over the years as their schedules allowed. The harpsichord Fergus had built here was still in the low, long sitting room; Helen had given it a thorough cleaning and waxing last week.

Well, to hell with it. Socks, socks, socks. The rubber boots had a leak in the left one: there weren't enough socks in the world to keep up with the wet. Damnit, she thought, if I were with the State Department I'd be getting hardship pay for this. She rummaged among Fergus's things, finding a heavy pair that, doubled under at the toes, would do for today until her own dried. Simon's letters and telegrams fluttered to the floor, she picked them up and sat on the edge of the bed.

"—There was a bit of a dither whether or not to have the baby's baptism after the wedding or before; once the order of events was decided (baptism the day afterward) everything was delightful. Lois and Bobby wrote most of their own liturgy, or rather borrowed it from Tagore, Gibran & Co., quite predictably. Lois of course refused to have her father 'give her away,' but George was so delighted his daughter was bothering to marry at all, particularly the baby's father and the nice chap that young Bobby is, that he was quite willing to forgo that bit. We all relaxed and enjoyed the chocolate fudge wedding cake; I did myself up proud the next day with the baby, smoke and full pontificals, much enhanced by Anthea's elegant cousin Elizabeth taking on another godchild (Fergus is her other). She is as lovely a widow as she was a bride; we're driving down to Edinburgh together and it'll be good to chew over old times. Two days there filling in at the Institute until Hamilton shows up; I should be back at Crumbles with any luck by the time this arrives. P.S. You might get at sanding the front corridor if you've finished in the front of the house; beware of letting Penner talk you into his men doing it. For what he'd ask for it I could put flagstone down."

Yes, well, getting the rented sanding machine to and from Canterbury would have been a great deal easier if Simon hadn't merrily gone off to the wilds of Scotland with the only set of his car's keys in his pocket. Helen had been dependent on sloshing into Harbledown on foot and taking taxis, since Simon refused to have a telephone in the house.

"Help. Trapped in God Factory. Visiting Roman Bishops. Staying Elizabeth's until Wednesday soonest."

Damn and blast. And then:

"Hamilton further delayed. Obliged continue his seminar until Friday. Remind electrician garden light. Simon." A *week* ago.

She flipped the papers back onto the dresser crates, hating herself for feeling catty, bitchy, and utterly sure that Anthea would have had closets full of dresser scarves, lampshades, little gay bits of this and that to brighten up this dank wreck. To say nothing of the fair Elizabeth— and all those nice old times they'd be remembering together while Helen was left down in waterlogged Kent to baby-sit on Mr. Penner, to brew endless pots of tea for "the lads," to find and lend wrenches to plumbers, trowels to masons, brushes to painters, pastepots to wallpaperers, wire cutters to electricians, crowbars to wreckers. The wonder of the week was that Mr. Penner had shown up this morning with his own ladders. But the day was young.

And to top it all off, Helen had quite literally varnished herself into these two small rooms, Fergus's desolate little bedroom and the old kitchen. After she had come to terms with the bucking and skidding and noise of the sanding machine and had stripped down the hallway floor that gave access to the rest of the house, it seemed a perfect chance to seal off the clean wide planks with the gallon of varnish that was said to be diamond hard and impervious to everything. It was guaranteed to dry within four hours; she distrusted that and moved a few of her old clothes into Fergus's room. Twenty-four hours would guarantee a really tough coat.

Three days later it was still wet, tacky. The charming and finally comfortable long sitting room with its new wallpaper, the books cleaned and rearranged on the new shelves, chimneys swept and fires laid, the windows reglazed, bits of freshly painted trim, polished brass, and comforting radio and music tapes, the great firm mattress on Simon's bed—all, all were beyond the damply varnished corridor, the windows and front door locked from within. To say nothing of her own toys, which would have kept her occupied: her cameras, contact prints and manuscript notes for a possible photographic essay were locked in a secret cupboard in the dining room. And above all, the major expense on the inside of the house, the new bathroom with its cheerful sparkle, vast tub and shower, and above all its hot-water heater, all, all impossible to reach unless she gave up on the floor. But to do so would mean either putting down plastic sheets, hell to get off later, or tracking wet varnish onto the nice old rugs and floors of the rest of the house.

"Must be a rum lot Simon got ahold of," Mr. Penner had noted with satisfaction. "Doesn't do not to have a professional at these things, we'd have spotted the trouble first off. Now I can send the lads over and have a proper job done by the time he's back—" Helen had declined; he would surely wreak some sort of punitive cost on top of the discouraging sum he was charging for everything else. Besides, it seemed a tiny bit drier this morning—perhaps.

And of course she'd been expecting Simon back long before this to decide what to do. After all, she may have laughingly given Crumbles its name a few years ago when she'd first seen it, but it wasn't her house or her budget, and she hadn't even particularly liked the color of the new bathroom. Why *did* men like maroon so much—bathrobes and cars and neckties and robes? Lugubrious. Anthea, she was sure, would have had pale blue. Bitchy, bitchy. As if in apology to Simon's dead wife, Helen began making the bed after all.

One day Fergus would surely put a shower into the little lavatory off the kitchen; since the fiasco of the varnish three days ago she'd managed with kettles of hot water. Kettles—the one she'd left on the kitchen stove began to whistle, then scream, simultaneously with a deep ominous groan from the ceiling above her; either Alf's or Ralph's legs descended a ladder outside the window.

Mr. Penner had abandoned the armchair by the little fireplace, leaving an empty bottle of ale by his cigar butt in the ashtray. But whatever he had gone outside for, it was definitely not time for his "lads" downing tools for tea yet. Helen made herself a pot of coffee and did what she could about toasting a stale piece of bread, hoping for a little more peace. Morning was not her season.

Was it the Madwoman of Chaillot who had one newspaper, carefully preserved, which she had found so perfect decades ago that she read it afresh every morning? The combination of an overdue suicide, a titillating duel, a rise on the Bourse, gossip of a famous demimondaine and her titled lover, a classic bal-masque, a divine weather forecast, the Prince de Galles in Paris for the opening of Longchamps, a marriage in Rome and an abdication in the Balkans—the wonderful old crazy had seen no need to look further for the perfect start to her day.

Today's *Times*, which Penner had left crumpled on the chair, looked from the front page an utter reverse to

Helen, who remembered that paper when it was staid, august, austere. Now it blazoned news of a Member of Parliament denying any impropriety in his recently exposed possession of a pied-à-terre furnished floor to ceiling and wall to wall in black leather. A Nazi war criminal had been kidnapped by the Israelis from hiding in North Africa. The dollar sagging disastrously one more time. An exhibition of Churchill paintings. An elderly widow's will, Mrs. Sarah Wilcox leaving her fortune to a son killed thirty-five years ago. Seventeen teenagers dead in a dance-hall fire in Aberdeen. A blind woman trapped for three days in a Manchester public library. Three Frenchmen kidnapped in the Sahara by the Algerians. An IRA bomb discovered in a hotel in Gibraltar—going a bit far afield these days, aren't they, she thought. All in all, pretty tacky; the Madwoman had the right idea.

The Court Circular, by contrast, was disappointingly dull. A Guild of Featherfluffers or something was giving the Duchess of Brede a luncheon today, but no news of the Royals. Undoubtedly they were huddling by their fireplaces watching television if they were wise. There was, however, the puzzle. She put down her coffee and, pushing her glasses up on her nose, reached for a pencil and got to work.

1 Down: To be flung. 3.

That was easy. It was ground into every crack and fissure of her mind. She quickly penciled the word in.

Mud.

Throwing the tea leaves from the third pot she'd made for Alf and Ralph's lunch into the garbage, she looked from the window and saw Mr. Penner had returned and was pulling on rubber boots from the trunk of his car, where his golf bag lay wrapped in a camel's hair blanket. He mounted one of the ladders and she heard him overhead, calling to one of the lads standing on the mangled

hydrangea plants below. Either Alf or Ralph closed his
open mouth and began to move one of the ladders; his
feet slipped and the ladder wavered faster and faster
sideways, fell slantwise against what sounded like the
kitchen chimney, which the sweep had refused to clean
until the roof was repaired. An enormous clot of soot,
stone, mortar fell down, spreading out a vast cloud of
black on the already filthy floor, stifling the last of the
coal fire, and garnishing Helen's toasted cheese sandwich
with the skeleton of a bat.

Oh Christ, Helen coughed, fumbling toward the window, to hell with the State Department. *Danger* pay from
the Army—even the C.I.A. would send a helicopter to get
me out of this.

She flung up the window, partly to rant at Mr. Penner
and partly to sneeze some of the soot out of her nose and
throat. Penner righted the ladder and clambered down
with agility, keeping his flashy coat somehow free of the
muddy rungs and taking a telegram from the boy who
had plowed up the drive on a bicycle, signing for it and
tipping the kid.

"Mr. Penner," she coughed, "would you care to take a
look in here and see what that did to the chimney and
fireplace?"

She drew back from the window, permitting him a
view. He handed her the telegram and peered in. The
soot was settling into small dunes in the damp air and lay
like vast ink splotches across most of the floor.

"Well, look at that indeed. Cleaned the chimney flue
for you, did it? Not to worry, Helen. No charge. No
charge at all."

At that moment the bedroom ceiling fell in.

"Well, you poor thing." Mrs. Ferrar, owner of the Mi-
tered Martyr, Harbledown's little inn, twirled the regis-
tration book around toward Helen, who stood forlornly in

front of the bar with duffel bags at her feet and soot and plaster on her face and hair. Alf and Ralph had obliged by bringing her away in the back of the truck; Mr. Penner's beige suede upholstery inside the Daimler was not offered.

Crumbles' thatch had been left covered in what looked to Helen like the world's largest Baggie, the thick plastic sheeting expertly weighted down and lashed against winter gales. One of the lads had crunched through the havoc inside and brought out Helen's things from Fergus's room; she'd locked the kitchen door and given Mr. Penner the key.

"I can't tell you what to do; Simon'll have to decide about that rotten beam or whatever it is. Good-bye, Mr. Penner."

The brass clock behind Mrs. Ferrar chimed three. "Of course we have a room, but I'm a wee bit afraid it's just for the night, dear. Chaucer Charabancs, you see, they book us full up every Friday to Monday and run the tours to Canterbury itself from here. It's only the two days ordinarily, but of course with the Royal Visit Sunday and Monday it's through Tuesday this time. I don't know what to suggest for tomorrow—perhaps one of the women in the village—"

"Oh, well, that's okay, Mrs. Ferrar. I'll go up to London tomorrow. Could I have a hot bath now, though, lots of hot water? We had quite a mess out there."

"My dear, I know, Penner was here a few minutes ago about the Rotary lunch next week and told me. Sounds frightful. Poor Father Bede, what a thing to come home to, will he be back soon? One of the Canons at the Cathedral rang up this morning trying to reach him—they were hoping he'd be able to go in and give them a hand during The Visit."

"I shouldn't think so, but I really don't know. I'd like to put in a call for him now at this number, and could I get some coffee and a sandwich? I seem to have missed lunch somewhere along the line."

"Of course, coffee and a cheese tart, that's what you need. I'll put the call in for you now, and have your bags taken up. There's a little fire in the parlor—I'll bring you a tray there and your bath will be ready just after."

Helen shucked off her sooty pea jacket; the pretty chintz on the chair by the fire was too nice to be smudged. What now? No telling, really, until she'd talked to Simon. If nothing else, he'd be quite into the old nostalgia gig with the fair Elizabeth, plus those bishops. Now, if Elizabeth were old enough to have been Fergus's godmother, she'd be just the right age for Simon, wouldn't she? And she'd have done all her homework over the years, all those nice cozy memories and associations and so forth. Besides, if he'd wanted any of those people to meet me he'd have taken me with him in the first place—

God bless crossword puzzles, they did take your mind off things and fill in the odd moment when you're in no shape to be thinking about anything at all. The telegram Penner had given her fluttered out from among the sheets of newsprint. What would it be this time? Simon's services desperately needed to judge a scone and bannock sale at— What are bannocks, anyway? They always sound like a horse disease—Elizabeth's church fair?

"There was a scone, too, dear, and jam," Mrs. Ferrar whispered as she set down a tray by Helen, "here's your key, dinner at seven-thirty. Oh, and your call to the Institute came through but Father Bede's gone and they hadn't a number."

"Hmm. I'm past being surprised. Thanks, Mrs. Ferrar." The innkeeper fluffed up her brassy hair and licked a bit of lipstick off her front teeth, pulled down her sweater, and went back to the bar. Helen attacked the coffee and tart, both of which were steaming hot and tasty, before idly opening the telegram.

Not a telegram after all, a cable.

BULLOCK C/O BEDE CRUMBLES HARBLEDOWN KENT ANGLETERRE WHOEVER WAS BURGLING YOUR APART- MENT NEW YORK WHEN I TELEPHONED MUST HAVE GONE THROUGH YOUR DESK BY THEN SINCE HE GAVE ME THIS ADDRESS SUITABLY TACKY TOO STOP WHAT ARE YOU DOING IN ENGLAND I THOUGHT BY NOW YOU HAD GIVEN UP TRYING TO GET THAT PRIEST UNFROCKED STOP HOW- EVER THAT IS YOUR PROBLEM STOP AM ON DEATHS DOOR- STEP AND KNOW YOU WOULD WISH TO SPEND MY LAST HOURS WITH ME AS I PLUCK FEVERISHLY AT THE COVER- LET STOP PERHAPS YOU CAN KEEP GRIM REAPER AT BAY STOP TO THIS END PAID TICKET YOUR NAME ROYAL AIR MAROC LONDON TAKE TAXI FROM AIRPORT TWENTY- FOUR DERB ZEMRANE BAB DOUKKALA MARRAKECH MEDINA PAY NO MORE THAN FIFTEEN DIRHAMS THEY WILL ASK FORTY STOP AM SINKING FAST STOP ARTHUR

Arthur! Arthur Bettman! My God, I haven't got a thing to wear. She laughed then, thinking how true clichés could be, but that had indeed been her first thought. Her real suitcases with dresses and shoes, as well as her cam- eras and so forth, were locked up in Crumbles. However, it didn't really matter, she would always have sartorial egg on her face in Arthur's eyes, and always had. They had grown up together in the summers, shared the same birthday and year, the same young rebellion from what was stuffy of the Midwest, thrashed about and survived and succeeded in their very different ways. Sometimes laughing, sometimes scratching, they had kept in touch, were—friends.

She had learned long ago to discount by half anything from Arthur; she'd once told him his patron saint must be

St. Hyperbole. Still, it wasn't a bit like him to ask for anything, much less her company at a sickbed. Marrakech—
what on earth could he have gotten there? Camel flu?
Sunstroke?

Sun. Oh, what a lovely thought. Morocco. No winter.
No rain. There wasn't anything more she could do here
for Simon; she'd lent her own apartment in New York
until New Year's to Russ Nolan, an old colleague from
their days together on the defunct *Globe*. He was trying
to decide between divorce or duty, poor man. Besides,
however jaunty Arthur sounded, he was miserly enough
so that the prepaid ticket should be taken into account.
His success as an architect hadn't offset the suspicion he
had always had that People Were After His Money,
suffered so often by those who had inherited fortunes. He
was a frightful tightwad about a lot of things, and perhaps the saddest were his affections. This silly cable was
the closest she'd ever, in long decades of knowing him,
heard him come to saying help.

And Simon was being so utterly exasperating. She
poked at the fire and, leaning back, opened the *Times*.
She wouldn't decide about anything until she'd had a
bath and dinner—of course not.

Chewing on the pencil, she let her gritty eyes run down
the clues. 15 Down. Bit of bread followed shows the
French path. 8-4. Well, there's that m in there from "dilemma." French was usually il or une—m blank une? No,
wait, m blank les? Ah, yes. Bit of bread.

Crumbles. Crumbles Away.

CHAPTER I

Sliding a bolt the size of a shotgun across the colossal doors that had banged shut on the darkening muddy street, the barefooted round little woman in layers of brocade, lamé, acetate glitter pulled Helen through a zig-zag hallway and across an enormous interior courtyard, rain dropping noisily on wet tiles and the leaves of orange and lemon trees. A central fountain repeated the plashing; almost sighs seemed to come from the four towering cypress trees in the corners.

Arthur lay at the end of a vast, high-ceilinged salon, its tiled walls lined with low banquettes and cushions interrupted only by a minuscule fireplace put where it would do the least possible good, directly opposite the huge drafty doors. He was heaped around with loose pillows, a ropy white turban wound around his head, and his long body wrapped in a flurry of white fluff interspersed with stripes of oversized loose silver sequins. The light from a television set in front of him cast a bright green on his face on one side; the glow of a bottled gas heater on wheels flickered orangely on the other.

He looked for all the world to Helen like a sick caterpillar dressed up for a party.

She dropped her pea jacket on the banquette by the door and wriggled out of her boots as he turned off the television. The rugs that lay ahead of her were too fine to muddy, and far warmer underfoot than the insides of the boots, which were still damp from Crumbles.

"Damnit, I'd forgotten there's no television here until evening. Godforsaken land." He groaned and lay back.

"Well, Arthur, hello—" Helen began; he waved a languid hand at her to push the television set away. She pulled up a low stool beside the round table laden with magazines, mineral waters, a brass-encased hand mirror, newspapers, bottles of medicines, tablets.

"What are you staring at?" He opened one eye balefully.

"You. I thought you looked green when I came in, but that was the tube. You're yellow!"

"From what do you think the word jaundice derives? *And* hepatitis; I told you in my cable that I was deathly ill. Now you see. Dr. Riad assures me daily the jaundice part has peaked and is passing, passing away, but I wonder." He picked up the mirror and peered in it doubtfully, shuddered, and put it back down. "Very, very depressing."

"Poor Arthur, it must be. How about this sawbones, Riad or whatever, is he good or do you want me to get you to Paris or London right away? There's space all this week—I asked at the airport."

"No, no, Riad is doing everything by the book. I called my own man in New York, of course, and he confirmed the treatment. Which is, aside from liver and vitamin and iron or whatever injections every day, simply rest rest rest. Now that may sound simple, but I'm so ill that even resting seems more than I can bear to do. Especially when I've got to live on yogurt and Vichy and a sliver of fish and boiled lettuce from time to time—I'm dying of starvation, but anything else is disaster."

"Poor thing. No booze either, I imagine. But then you never were much of a drinker."

"No, but I enjoyed every wee drop. When I think of what a little champagne can do for a headache, or flu—and this is so much worse. Worse carried to the ninth power, with no pick-me-up possible—kif is *not* the same, I assure you—I dream of ginny in a light brown glass . . ." His dolorous hum died out weakly.

"Where'd you get it, when and how?"

"Spain, perhaps, the deadly *maruescos* of Marbella. Finishing that villa after all; the owners got rich again suddenly, so we got the foundations out of mothballs and the thermopane windows and sauna and hot tub and so forth out of customs and the bricklayers back from the fleshpots of Palm Beach or wherever they go on their astronomical salaries. Very nice job it is, too; I came down here for rest, sun, fun—and also to find some carpets for the owners. Don't ever let anyone talk you into the *soi-disant* mild winters of the Costa del Sol—gelid isn't the word. Of course the thing had had an iron grip on my liver for three weeks before without my knowing it. I succumbed the day after I got here—what is it, two weeks ago."

"Oh, dear. Well, for one thing you're bound to lose weight without even trying, which is always nice—maybe this whole thing'll be a sort of pre-penance for all kinds of excess when it's over."

"Ever the Pollyanna. At our age getting thin is very very tricky, Helen. A flat tummy is good, yes, but then inevitably it's accompanied by scraggly necks and hollow faces. Don't know which is worse." He peered at Helen suspiciously as if she might have found some solution he hadn't. "Ah, here is Hecate with her afternoon brew." The maid had added a green and gold knitted scarf to the magenta chiffon binding her head; the shimmering patterns of layers of caftans, tucked up in front into a gold-embroidered belt, reflected in the mirroring brass of the round, short-legged tray which she beamingly carried and set on the table.

"Zohra, *je voudrais te presenter mon amie Helen. Elle va rester ici pendant quelque jours comme je t'ai dit ce matin.*" Zohra's plump warm hands pressed Helen's and she was kissed roundly on both cheeks, the maid flashing a smile of golden teeth. From somewhere in the upper folds of her garments she whipped out a stick of incense, lit it, and stuck it firmly into a small raw potato on the tray, smiling again as she scurried out, the light revealing intricate lacy henna designs on her feet and hands.

"They swear the incense makes you feel warmer. Snuff it out, will you? Orchid Orgasm isn't really my thing. She's a witch you know, not a maid at all."

"Really? How can you tell?" Helen was peering into the two teapots on the tray, each with a ruby and gold glass beside it.

"These brews, these brews. Not yours, yours'll be the one with the green slime swimming around, mint actually. Mine is the telling one, a potion of oregano, Lysol, honey, kif, thyme, *eau de javel*, dead steeped lizard, and pounded cowrie shells no doubt. So utterly vile you get better if only never to have to drink it again as long as you live. Pour it out the window behind you, will you, and give me some of yours. You'll get along with Zohra all right in French, by the way, so ask her for anything you want. There's a scullion of sorts around too, one of her familiars, of course, although she *says* it's her daughter. By the way, I hope you brought something to wear?" He peered over the gold rim of the tea glass at her pullover and corduroy pants. "You're a bit damp, aren't you? I smell wet dog."

"Damp, yes, and dog, no; it's the wool that smells that way. Clothes. Not really. I was in the country." No point going into the scene at Crumbles, the things that were locked up there wouldn't count as clothes to Arthur, and Royal Air Maroc had lost her duffel bags en route from London. All she had were a few things in a carry-on bag, socks and a nightgown and so on. "I hoped I could find something here. Floating caftans?"

"Helen, nobody wears floating caftans here—and you're

not the type to wear them anywhere. We'll have to get you something. Won't need much, of course. I don't see you in with the jet set, somehow—it's more the propeller set actually, but still they do dress. However, you don't play bridge either, so that's out. There are a few amusing people, though—a bit young, but you'll have to manage. With no clothes and your French it's all I can come up with."

"I concede the clothes, and of course my French leaves much to be desired, but I've gotten round the world with its help more than once."

"I'm sure you have, but this isn't round the world. This is Marrakech. However, since I don't see you in with the Gaudy Gueliz Gangsters—Gueliz is the French town outside the ramparts—anyway, you'd have to change costumes five times a day, slander in a suitable accent, and tooth and claw your way into the society of a bunch of alcoholic old queens who do nothing but drink and steal each other's boyfriends, who in turn steal all of them blind—no, I'll turn you over to Erica, she knows everybody that'd be comfortable with you."

"You don't need to worry about amusing me, I came down to pat your brow with eau de cologne, you know. I'll be quite happy just mooching around seeing the sights; it all seems much busier and more prosperous than I remembered."

"Oh, yes, you were here for that earthquake in Agadir, weren't you. I should have remembered. All those dead bodies and our Helen with her brownie. When was that?"

"Sixty. And I did get this far for the Marche Verte in seventy-five, but I was plucked out untimely and replaced by Hellmer—irritating, but they were probably right that a man would do better in Islam."

"Spare me the details, I should have known. Perhaps I can arrange a nice gory revolution or a little cholera epidemic for you this time." He closed his eyes and lay back, holding the little tea glass in both hands on his abdomen. "Do something about that wretched little fire, I'm cold."

Helen got up and found a deep copper vat full of gnarled olive-wood logs; she added several, but the dim, painted wooden ceiling was so far above and the tiles radiated so much damp it would make no effect.

"Where, by the way, are we? A friend's house?"

"Here? Oh, it belongs to some sort of jack-of-all-trades type, a Balt or Estonian or Finn or something. Latvian, that's it. Gleb Kauder. He's been here for decades, doing a bit of this, a bit of that, collecting things, although that must have been a long time ago when they were available for nothing. Likes to rent this place when a good tenant comes along; he goes down to the desert with his sand shovel and bucket, God knows what. He popped in from somewhere this morning, brought me the papers from Gueliz, very thoughtful, but he's off again, you've missed him. Better for me here than the Mamounia, I can tell you. If I have to be ill I'll be damned if I'll pay their prices, for one thing. Might as well be wretched here where there are a few pleasures for the eye. Whoever redecorated that hotel has the soul of a Belgian house-wife. Utterly ruined. Besides, I've never stayed in an Arab house; interesting. Ghastly acoustics, no closets, dashing through the weather from room to room—still, there's something. Ah, here's my fix, and just in time."

Accompanied by Zohra, a very tall, very black man who, Helen thought, should have a dagger between his teeth and a rose behind his ear, burst sideways into the room, scuffing off yellow pointed slippers and flinging back a felt burnoose theatrically, spattering raindrops about him. Arthur made an effort toward hunching himself up from the pillows, knocking his turban slightly awry. "Helen—SiOmar."

The little devil, Helen thought as he pressed her hand

unmistakably between both of his warm, strong, dry palms. He *is* kind of cute, and doesn't he know it.

"Ah, Madame, welcome in Marrakech! You are to come to us for the Great Feast—L'Aid el Kebir—in some days. You must to come to him. I kill sheep *moi-même* with knife. *C'est très très beau, le sacrifice, très important pour vous à voir.*"

"*Merci bien, monsieur.* I've never been here for your holiday before. Thank you for inviting me."

"Should be just your thing, Helen." Arthur was rolling over and unswathing himself from his wrappings. "For one thing, it's the only place you'll get anything to eat— the witch and her familiars'll be scurrying off to their coven for the day and I doubt you'll want to fend in what they call a kitchen. And all that throat-slitting—you'll love it." He was wrenching his pajama bottoms down over one hip.

"Arthur, I'll go up or down or wherever and find my room—I want some dry socks for one thing. Can I bring you anything later?"

"No, nothing. Come back about eight for your dinner here; then the telly. Soap opera. AS THE THIRD WORLD TURNS. Will Yusuri survive the magic his mother-in-law Toumia is brewing against him so that her daughter Habiba can marry Jalal? Will L'Hassan be able to pay the rent for his hanout in the brass souk? If not, will he and Qamar return to the farm with the children?"

"I can hardly wait," she grinned. "*Le fête,* SiOmar, *c'est pour quelle jour?*"

"Ah, this we do not know exactly, *chère* Madame." He waved a hypodermic needle grandly in an arc with one hand, the other seizing Helen's and pressing it to his knowing kiss. "*Mais je crois en trois, quatre jours.* Lalla Kinza go home, which is *mzyan bzef parceque* I more beautifuler cook than *elle.* The short boys be happy you our guest. *D'accord?*"

"*D'accord* by me." As she picked up her jacket she hoped that whatever was going to happen would find her warmer and readier to face a gaggle of short boys, whoever they might be.

She had no trouble finding the room upstairs she was to occupy. The little "familiar" seemed not to speak any French, but sweetly kissed Helen's hand and carried the kiss, with its baraka, back to her own face, then led her up steep stairs to a high dark room with a mattress and bolster on the floor, a dreary French armoire, and Helen's small bag, illuminated by what must have been a two-watt lightbulb inside a red glass lantern high on the ceiling, and by what was left of the light from the fading wet afternoon from a grilled small window opening onto the gallery. All singularly cheerless. Cheerless was the large formal garden below the gallery, cheerless the lights in the little windows opposite her own on the other side of the garden. Padding out onto the gallery in Fergus's damp socks, she entered a series of various-sized connecting rooms stretching over the salon in which Arthur lay downstairs. They housed shelves and tables and cabinets of a jumbled collection of ceramics, bins of silver jewelry mixed with loose beads of coral, amber, amazonite. Ancient caftans of green, apricot, black, laden with gold embroidery, hung from open chests. Slippers, swords, knives, muskets inlaid with mother-of-pearl, powder horns, water bottles lay about among savage rugs hung from the walls or tumbled in bales on the floors.

Looking forward to seeing the owner's goodies in better light tomorrow, she followed the open doorways and arches to a small room at the end. Aha, the plumbing! Very basic it was, but there was a hot-water heater, thank heaven, attached to a bottle of gas.

The room with the lighted windows across from hers was Arthur's—clearly the owner's room. The ubiquitous

tiles here had been covered by simple white cloth hangings; on the wall opposite the bed hung an exquisite mat
of thin threads of leather and bamboo. Odd, dull indigos,
burgundies, saffrons. Too old and fine by far to grace a
floor any longer; it also had a distinct look of the other
side of the Sahara. But Helen was more immediately interested in Arthur's Butagaz heater on wheels, turned on
full blast, and a serious bedside lamp. She peeled off the
socks and hung them in front of the heater, sticking her
feet into Arthur's enormous fleece-lined slippers and
squatting down for a serious look at the bookshelf. She'd
bought at least a dozen paperbacks at Heathrow, but they
were in her lost luggage. She curved her neck to read the
spines, hoping against hope. Arabic, Arabic, of course, but
—English! Lots! At least a dozen old Nevil Shutes, and
Maugham, Dick Francis, MacLean, Van Druten. She felt
an upsurge of faith that she would somehow survive. Especially since there was a London *Times* on Arthur's table
downstairs, the same one she'd been doing the puzzle in
when she left England. Artist follows horse. 5. Artist, that
was always Royal Academy—oh, of course, Cobra.

"I think it's by order of Mohammed—or Allah himself,
what does it matter? Every family is supposed to slaughter or sacrifice a sheep in memory of Abraham and Isaac,
and there's a lot of visiting and eating and sheer gorging
for three days." Arthur looked up from his bowl of clear
broth and dish of plain rice at Helen's dinner, which she
was eating with her fingers in the absence of any cutlery.
It was exquisitely odorous of lamb, cinnamon, honey, al-
monds.

"I see—like Easter or Christmas, or both together."

"Well, I give you Christmas, with all the swilling.
What's Easter in it?"

"The sacrifice. Yourself anew, I should think."

"Ghastly way to look at it, but I leave theology to you.

Pretty hard lines on little Isaac, I do think. That boy must have been a mass of complexes the rest of his life. Sarah was supposed to have been a looker, to begin with, so I'm sure the lad had the hots for Mama just like all little boys, and there's Daddy Abraham with a knife at the child's throat. No angel appeared in time to prevent A Great Deal of Damage Being Done, Helen. I'll bet you anything Isaac ended up queer as Dick's hatband."

"Perhaps. Oh, how I wish you could eat some of this, it's too unctuous for words. Now, who is this SiOmar and the short boys and all?"

"SiOmar is a functionary of some sort in a rehabilitation center here for crippled boys. Polio, MS, TB of the bone, you name it and they have it. One of those Garrison Centers, they're all over. SiOmar does some commonsense physiotherapy and nursing, teaches the little buggers leather craft, weaving, shoemaking, and so forth. He and the Peace Corps girl who is the nominal head of it alternate in giving me my daily *piqures*—Erica got them organized for me."

"I see. Very handy. And who—"

"Before you come to that, you'll be having a ladies' lunch tomorrow—Little Miss Twinkletoes, Debbysue—no, it's real—Debbysue Kemp is the Peace Corps girl and she's coming to take you to lunch at Erica's. Now, Erica Portland is a very useful person to know, I assure you. In the first place she can provide some clothes for you, since that's her métier, and the sooner the better." He glared at Helen's sweater and pants. She retaliated by popping a particularly succulent piece of lamb into her mouth.

"She must be useful, finding you a house and nurses and doctors and garbing my ancient bod and all."

"Yes. I advise you to like her. She even organized the wine you're drinking so much of—no, no, keep at it, there's more. Although if I recall correctly it's rather second-rate. What you've got to remember is that anything that's reasonably good here is far better someplace else. Snow for skiing, brief and unpredictable. Beaches, undertow. Arts and crafts, utterly corrupted. Food, either feast or famine, with no sane daily delight. Roads, passable, but where do they lead? Climate, either freezing or roasting, with not as much of that wondrous spring and fall as travel agents let you believe. And on top of it all, or perhaps the very best indication of how second-rate it all is, even the *missionaries* are tacky—Jehovah's Witnesses or something."

"Arthur, that has to be your liver talking. I remember some pretty stupendous scenery, if nothing else."

"Well, keep remembering it, because it'll be your only solace. Now, after tomorrow's luncheon with the girls I'm giving a little dinner the night afterward—there are some people you have to meet."

"This is ridiculous." She set her glass down. "You're ill and bright yellow and I'm here to fill your hot-water bottles or read aloud from Beatrix Potter, and now you're practically giving a debut for me. I can amuse myself, this is too silly, all these parties."

"Ah, but it's work work work all the time in my head, dearie, and yours too. This dinner is in aid of Arthur and Arthur only, as I shall make clear. I want you to meet Stanley Overton—you've heard of him, Lord Overton, Overton Enterprises, everything from Advertising to Zwieback and any business in between. Good works, of course, a director of the Garrison Centers, Churchill buff, get the boys out of the slums clubs. You're to make him a constant companion, if not best friend, as soon as possible. His lady wife Neva is coming along next week, but he's here now and I want you to start to work on him as soon as possible. Confined to my couch as I am, you must scamper about for me. Fortunately—well, I can't see them in those things you're wearing, but scampering is to your advantage, since your legs are one of your better remaining points."

"I see. All becomes sickeningly clear. You have a project?"

"I have a project. I want to know if Overton is commissioning me to build him a villa here plain and simple—although it won't be plain or simple, of course—or if I am to be included in the plans he has with the 'Mystery' of Liaison and Development, in the person of the Minister himself, to build a few little hotels of grand luxe in this benighted country. I can usually read a client's mind with one eye closed, but there's something evasive, unclear, in all this. For one thing, there seems to be no plan for a hotel in Marrakech; now that the Mamounia's taking in tour buses—they say they don't, but *I've* seen them hidden across the street—something like the *old* Palais Jamai in Fès comes to mind. Too bad that's been torn down. Well, it's all too iffy—the villa's a sure thing, but this other's being—dangled. It may not come off."

"Sounds like a lot of work."

"That wouldn't bother me—like you, I thrive on it. But if not, I want to know soon, because there's that vulgar Arab who's bought Long Island, he'll surely want a new palace there and I should be wooing him instead. So you see, I look to you to sniff around and go places, or at least see these people with your eyes and ears open."

"Oh, dear, I should have known, shouldn't I?"

"Of course. Why should you mind? You can't tell me you were having such a stellar time at that parson's wallow in Kent, anyway. You look frightful. Do you good to get tarted up and move about with reasonably stylish types for a change. Besides, you really are the only person I could think of with nothing to do anyway who I could trust. I'm counting on you. This isn't all holiday, you know."

Helen thought of the cold, uncomfortable room upstairs with not enough blankets on the bed, of her clumsy boots waiting at the door and the rain-washed garden with the dripping trees, of planning her mad dash across it to the stairs without getting more than one spurt of water down the back of her neck. Of the tepid water that trickled thinly into the tub after the explosive boom of the hot-water heater turning on. Of Arthur's bedroom, with the electric blanket and the gas heater and the beautiful mat and all the books. Of Arthur now, wrapped snugly in his spangled fluffy wool, the heater glowing and the television turned squarely toward him, leaving her to listen to the dialogue in Arabic.

"No, Arthur, it most very certainly is not."

CHAPTER II

"Oh, goody, I was afraid you mightn't have clothes and we'd have to take a taxi." Debbysue Kemp looked approvingly at Helen's garb as they pulled the street doors of Gleb Kauder's house behind them and set off down the narrow street. "Arthur looks real well this morning—I stopped off to say hello before you came down. You must have been here in the wintertime before, I guess—everybody else shows up with little old sunsuits and sandals."

"More luck than experience; I was in England in the country when Arthur sent for me. I must say I'd hoped a change of clothes would be needed, but it's much the same."

"Frying pan into the fire, isn't it? Well, I hope the worst is over for today, anyway. That old sun is trying to come out. Course we'll have the mud until March at least. You don't mind walking, do you? I've got some errands in the souks and they're on the way down to the Center anyway. Arthur wants you to see it."

"I'd love it, souks and all. It's been ages since I've been here, and never with enough time to explore. Lead on." Helen thought she'd known what to expect when Arthur had told her this Peace Corps girl would take her to lunch at Erica's today: long hair, wire-framed glasses, earnest freckled face, Frye boots. Debbysue, however, was right out of *Mademoiselle*, springy golden hair well cut under her sou'wester, neat square handbag, strong yellow slicker and glistening rubber boots. The whole outfit probably came from J. C. Penney, these kids were paid peanuts, but it was saucy, well cut, and very feminine indeed. Just like the girl herself.

"Now, if you need a landmark,"—she pulled Helen back from sudden death as a pair of horses drawing a large black calèche full of veiled women clattered at a fast trot around the corner of the street they were entering, flinging mud on all sides as the driver's whip flicked the brim of the girl's sou'wester—"this restaurant here, Dar Toubkal, everybody knows where it is, so just ask for that, turn right, and you're home." A grim-faced and disillusioned doorman sat on a low stool in the dusky entryway; the glower on his face more than offset his richly embroidered costume and tasseled tarboosh. Helen thought it would take a more than usually persuasive tour guide to persuade his flock that they wouldn't have their throats cut before dessert. However, the wood-and-brass door sported enough credit-card and tour-group stickers to efface half the intricate carving. And after all, mystery in the medina was what middle-aged Belgians came to Marrakech for in the long run. They'd love it. Especially at night, scurrying in huddles under the low brick archways, with a dead cat or two in the corners to scandalize them, the blank windowless walls of the houses holding sulky secrets behind their dull rose plaster.

"If you-all haven't been there and want a night when Arthur feels better, Dar Toubkal's kind of pretty. It used to be a private house, really like a palace, but the family— they're awful rich—moved out of the medina after Independence. They've got a big place in Gueliz now, real French or whatever, swimming pool and air conditioning and all that. At least they didn't let this turn into a tenement or fall down like so many folks do as soon as they get enough money to get out. The owner—he's a friend of mine—owns just about all this neighborhood, too; he's making a pile from the restaurant. Now, if you see anything you want I can help with the haggling if you don't speak Arabic. Prices are just a scandal anymore."

They left behind the reasonably quiet bustle of women, shopping baskets akimbo, suspiciously sniffing carrots and turnips through their veils, children drawing buckets of water, little girls with trays of bread balanced on their heads scurrying to and from the public ovens, pairs of old men holding hands trustingly, purposeful young men on Mopeds weaving their buzzing way through the crowds, mint sellers with cloudy, blind eyes and their fine old hands endlessly rearranging their aromatic green bunches.

They plunged into a lattice-covered street redolent with the universally soothing smell of wood shavings, basket rushes, little grass-seated stools, boys at foot-powered lathes turning cedarwood for lattices. Then the acrid stench of metal, copper being pounded, brazed, polished, beaten; giant grindstones being turned by calloused feet while tools threw off bits of themselves in sparks from dark cubicles, ancient bellows insisting the glowing coals stay the color of a luminous gladiola on the clay pit in the floor of other shops.

A few minutes later Helen, sliding in the layer of mud overlying stone bricks worn down by the centuries into glassy smoothness, found Debbysue's bright slicker almost indistinguishable against the background of narrow small shops full from floor to ceiling with yellow pointed-toed slippers, looking for all the world like slices of stacked melon. Handcarts, one step ahead of the square wheel in design, caromed downhill dripping blood from stinking fresh hides; veiled women with arrogant and unbecoming billowing hoods topping their long tight djellabas brandished bunches of mint for noonday teapots. More slipper shops, these for the women, velvet *babouche* embroidered with gold. A piece of latticework above came loose and let a splat of water sting the crown of Helen's head as she dodged out of the way of an overladen donkey, ricocheting back against a man with no nose. Downward, the street widened, joined by a tributary fork, became more crowded. A string of tourists beat their way upstream with white, exhausted faces, shivering in thin raincoats and cotton dresses, wearing Suntours badges on their lapels and panic on their faces as they momentarily lost sight of their guide.

"If it's a gaggle of geese, could we have a terror of tourists?" Helen asked. Debbysue grinned with her beautiful American teeth and led her around a corner into a shop whose portico was decked with dried and stuffed lizards, hedgehogs, gnarled roots and bunches of herbs, strings of square brass amulets, bins of white quartzlike stones, jars of cowrie shells, unknowable dried leaves of presumed virtue. "Forget about getting any musk in *this* hanout, it's all fake here. But his saffron's good and makes a swell present at home, it's so cheap. Want some?"

Helen thought of Simon, the condition of the kitchen at Crumbles. But what the hell, saffron would keep. "Sure, I'd love a gram—does that sound right? I don't cook much myself, but a friend does."

The merchant was scooping up the wonderful soap of the countryside, thick and iridescently black, looking like tar and molasses, but smelling of the olives from which it was made. Debbysue chattered away with him as he weighed out her purchases, began the bargaining for the saffron, which he was pinching out of a large jar. Helen stepped out of the entrance and lit a cigarette, remembering an odd landmark or two in the little square with low trees, handcarts laden with towels for sale. Yes, that was it, the rug souk was down at the end through that small arch. She'd try to get back here one day soon and look for something for Crumbles. Or maybe not for Crumbles. The savage Berber designs would overwhelm the Anthea aspects of the place, which Helen hadn't known if Simon kept because he wanted them, or because they were, quite simply, there. To hell with Crumbles. She'd get one for herself; there were enough dark bare floors at Twelfth Street to welcome and set off anything she brought home. Including herself. Arthur was promising to be so disagreeable she wished Russ Nolan and his marital problems were someplace else and that she had the option of going back to New York sooner. In any event, it was time she did something to the old apartment. Now that she was there more and more it'd be fun to have some nicer things around her, get rid of that hideously Fifties wrought-iron table by her bed, for one thing.

Debbysue was putting her purchases into an iridescent peacock blue string bag; Helen gladly let the girl stow the saffron in with her own things and wished the dead lizards had more oomph, charm. She'd love really funny ones for Simon, for Arthur.

Turning back into the main street, they found the smell now was of cloth—brocades and tissues and rayons and lamés, gabardines, acrylics—every possible color and pattern in the world seemed to be hanging or floating or unrolled from laden shelves. Poles jutted out high above, flying gaudy caftans and the dafinas that went over them, sleazy blouses, gay little knee-length ruffled knickers. Eye-wincing shops full of new rugs so chemically colored they pierced the gloom of flyspecked forty-watt lightbulbs.

Pushing against the crowds, they fought under an arch and out into a long block of grain sellers in cavelike shops with waist-high fire pits, the air enticing with the smell of roasting chick peas, sunflower seeds, peanuts. Sacks of rice, lentils, millet, wheat, popcorn, cornmeal, couscous slumped on counters in the lattice-dappled light.

"Not far now—you okay?" Debbysue marched ahead briskly, swinging the bright blue net bag, to which she had added a new basket, half a dozen pairs of slippers for herself and three for Helen, tooled leather folders, wooden spoons, tiny jars of kohl. "I'm going home for good next week, you see, and I've got a *lot* of cousins, let me tell you." Helen herself had felt one of those inexplicable surges of glee in spite of the cold, the fatigue unlessened this morning by Zohra's glass of hot milk with—at the most—three grains of Nescafé in it and, at the least, six sugar cubes. She had fallen into the fun of the shopping, the young girl's cheer and good manners and enthusiasm, letting Debbysue with her Southern-belle charm bargain hard and shrewdly and utterly beguilingly with the merchants. When they left one shop the poor man had seemed not to have known what had happened, except that he had gained only a fifth of the money he'd expected to get from two ladies who should have been tourists.

"Well, d'you remember this, the great old Djemma el Fna of song and story?" They came out into the open at last, past an abrupt change through a bazaar of pottery and shabby brass belts and sleazy handbags.

"Oh, yes, I know where I am now—I think I remember the blind men, and there's the Café de France. But good lord, the traffic! It's like Times Square!"

"I've never been to New York except to change planes at Kennedy, but in my four years here I swear the number of cars and Mopeds triples every six months. You used to be able to sit in the old café and have a conversation. Can't hear yourself think now." Debbysue shook her head at the parking lot that faced the café, and grimaced as a demuffled Moped roared by. "Too bad it's so dismal today, not much of a welcome for you." The vast L-shaped *place* was not indeed beguiling at the moment; in the distance one hardy snake charmer had spread his plastic tablecloth over a rain puddle and was prodding a sluggish cobra who, however, clearly preferred to remain under a nice dry tambourine. Without customers, the long rows of stalls full of atrociously made shirts and gowns for the tourists straggled toward a row of low buildings, like a defeated and retreating army.

"Can you hang in until I get just a couple more last things?" Debbysue turned to a handcart laden with incense sticks, rough little bins of resin, myrrh, and frankincense, cheap brass burners. Helen put a coin into the bowl of the nearest blind man; she remembered vaguely someone telling her the same nine men had sung prayers with their empty bowls in that place for decades. Or at least nine men—surely not the same ones? Their milky or absent eyes bound them together, as did their imploring chant extolling generosity.

"There now, that's just *absolutely all,* I promise. You're sure one patient lady."

"Nonsense, I love it." They ambled past a busload of German matrons who were holding skimpy gowns from the stalls against their Wagnerian bosoms and wondering, wondering, being given no help by each other and too much from the brash young men in the stalls.

One lone scribe huddled beneath a rusty black umbrella; he was putting the cap on his bottle of Waterman's blue ink and packing his papers and notebooks into a wooden box. "We're almost there now." The call to midday prayer sang out from the tower of the Koutoubia mosque ahead of them, a flag fluttering from the summit. Noon. A definite feeling of closing up, waiting families, meals, the morning's work over. Helen was suddenly very hungry.

"So, here we are!" After a mad dash through traffic, all vehicles blowing their horns incessantly and donkeys tangling with bicycles, they had reached the low rosy walls of several small buildings run together, a blue grilled window and door, and hurried around the corner, the looming square tower of the Koutoubia directly in front of them. "Just aim for the old tower and you can't get lost. If you need a ladies' room or anything just bang on the

door and come in anytime." Passing by a plaque blazoned
with "Garrison Center" and a nail-studded blue door, she
pushed open a wrought-iron grille that led through a narrow passage open to the sky and overfull with a plastic-
sheeted wheelchair and a damp Moped.

The brightly tiled courtyard beyond was bare of plants,
trees, or amenity except for a pool in the corner, too large
and deep to be ornamental and a bit small for swimming.
It was empty except for a large ram quietly munching on
fodder, its hooves in a puddle of water. The drain was
clogged with straw, blown bits of leaves, tangerine peels,
paper. There were smears of mud and dirt on the ramp
that led into the pool, as if the sheep might have tried to
leave but found it too slippery; a frazzled rope had been
laced into a mesh of sorts across the handrail.

"Our new exercise pool, it's great for the boys' therapy
when it's warm—oh, phooey—duck inside while I stuff this
junk upstairs with my other things." Debbysue glittered
up a dark flight of stairs and Helen hurried from a fresh
spurt of rain into a dusky unlit room behind the closest
door. It was lined with narrow low cots covered with
black-and-yellow print bedspreads, a frank little low uri-
nal unscreened in one corner. A small boy lay on a cot
sucking his thumb and staring unseeingly at a pair of
leather and metal braces unstrapped on the bed beside
his twisted legs. The child responded to Helen's hello and
smile by wriggling deeper into the cot and closing his
eyes.

From somewhere through the series of connecting
rooms she smelled food, the stabbing odor of onions cooking, a distantly familiar spice, heard the clatter of women
kitchening.

She was swept with a sudden poignant nostalgia, nostalgia for now, for this moment. Not déjà vu, but the sure
knowledge that somewhere ahead in her life she would be
precipitated suddenly into a memory of this very moment

when she stood in a quiet, ugly room in a center for
crippled children in the middle of Marrakech, a small boy
on a cot and a sheep in a swimming pool and the smell of
onions and cumin—that was the spice, cumin—in the air.
How very odd, for there was nothing exceptional in the
moment itself—even the sheep in the pool, she knew, was
intended for the sacrifice in a few days. The garish bed-
covers were predictably institutional make-do, a remnant
of some second-rate hotel's curtains, perhaps. The very
important Victorian buffet with the cracked mirror in the
next room, and the three imitation Biedermeier chairs
around a table with cracked oilcloth on it would be dona-
tions from some departing colonist. Still, she shivered
suddenly. A goose walks on my grave—

"L'Hamdullah! Royal Air Maroc does have a place for
me! I've been trying to get out of here for three or four
months now, but something always comes up, and I get
the feeling when I change reservations these days they
think I'm just kidding anymore. Come on into the kitchen
and meet Lalla Kinza, she's housemother and cook and
just about everything else, and then we'll get on over to
Erica's." Debbysue led Helen through the little dining
room and down three damp steps into the kitchen. Helen
was smothered in a warm flurry of sleeves and scarves
and arms and kisses; Kinza was vast in height, volume,
and wardrobe. She and Debbysue were laughing at something, jabbering away in such fast Arabic it sounded like
perforations being torn off a spiral notebook.

"Lookit here what Lord Overton brought Lalla Kinza
from London!" Debbysue was putting a pair of huge
rhinestone-studded sunglasses on the cook's vast face;
Kinza began singing and swaying back and forth, dancing
with her arms and shoulders and laughing at the same
time. "She says she looks just like Om Kalsoum—you
know, the Egyptian torch singer. She does, too. That was
darling of him—things like this cost a fortune here. Last
year he brought all the boys Garrison Center T-shirts,

they were wild over them. And he's got a super treat for the left-behinds for L'Aid—oh, dear, I wish he'd let me know he was going to be here this morning. Kinza says he's been here going over papers in the office upstairs all morning, and I never get a chance to mix much wit de quality. A real Lord.

"Come along, I'll give you a quick look at the crafts room," she continued. "This is where old SiOmar—hey, he's just mad about you, by the way—teaches the kids shoemaking and weaving. They eat in here, too." The low worktable and small benches on either side were cleanly wiped, the wall shelves held supplies and samples neatly, but the floor had snippets of leather, crumbs of bread and orange peel, tufts of wool wherever it would take more than a casual hand to clean. They looked quickly into the schoolroom beyond; a thin young man on crutches was teaching a handful of very small boys French, *"le chameau"* nicely drawn on the blackboard. Like small boys anywhere they turned and wiggled and stared and giggled at Helen from their footstool-height desks; they were all sitting on triangular skateboard affairs, their legs like withered pretzels.

"All the others—we've usually got twenty-five—have all gone home this morning for L'Aid. It's usually a madhouse just before lunch. His lordship must have been in here too—all those marvelous Pentel pens weren't here this morning. What a nice man. Well, these little ones, and Abdellatif, the teacher, they're all orphans so they're staying here—SiOmar's just impossible, he's so excited you're going to come for the sacrifice and all, Kinza's going home to her own family for the first time in years, so he'll rule the roost for three whole days. But you can see more of it later. I'm starving, let's get on to Erica's."

Erica Portland's hair swung down like a copper bell as she leaned forward over her worktable, pushing scraps and swatches of cloth to one side. She pulled forward the neat square basket with its blue cloth label stenciled in henna

Sur Commande
7 Derb Demnat
Kasbah
Marrakech-Medina

and looked with dubious satisfaction at the silk kimono folded attractively inside. She'd bought it from a desperate Japanese hippie last spring, the kid had wanted money for hash, of course, and had taken the fifty dirhams she'd offered. The dull silk was in perfect condition, thick and rich; she'd only had to cut down the sleeves a bit, add pockets, and give it to SiMohammed, her tailor and a master in the country's fine art of weaving seams together with floss. He had opened every seam and finished them in a funky mulberry color, the color contrasting beautifully against the maroon silk. The only question now was how much she could get from Stanley Overton for it. Five hundred dirhams? Seven hundred and fifty? Too little—anything comparable in London would easily be a hundred pounds. And he was on a holiday, in a spending mood.

She slipped a card on which she'd written "Stanley, What do you think of this Moroccan kimono? Perfect for you, no?" into the neckline. He'd take it like a shot, and she could wait and put the price in with his wife's bill after Neva had come in next week and placed her usual large order. She'd drop this off at the Mamounia for Stanley on her way to Bettman's dinner tomorrow. Overton was compulsively punctual and if she were a few minutes late for dinner he wouldn't run into her at the desk and assume—rightly—that she was saving a few dirhams by delivering it herself. Or that she were chasing him. Bad idea, that, for him to get just now. She'd deliberately waited this whole week for him to see her; yesterday he'd come in at last and they had begun thinking about his wife's "fiftieth" birthday present. A few more years than that, Erica smiled to herself, but what did it matter. He wanted one superb of everything, he'd said: necklace, bracelet, ring, caftan, slippers, belt—damn difficult in such a short time, finding anything old and beautiful, and Neva was so tiny as well she'd simply drown in some of the massive jewelry that Erica could get her hands on quickly. But it was all meant to be ready in time for that Churchill painting party in a few weeks' time. She'd simply have to manage somehow. Thank heaven for Gleb.

She could hear Fatima in the garden below her window, going ker-thunk ker-thunk ker-thunk on the washboard, and in her mind's eye could see that corner by the kitchen awash with piles of wet laundry, soaking, hanging, being scrubbed. Well, it was only old Debbysue and that American who needed clothes that were coming for lunch, it didn't matter today—but one day she'd put in some negotiable steps to the roof and have all the laundry done up there out of sight.

Oh no, she caught herself up, lighting a cigarette and looking in the long mirror with the chipped edge concealed by a swatch of Fès embroidery. You're getting out of this place, that's what you're doing. Not one more cent goes into this house. She pulled her subtle orange paisley shawl tighter around her straight lean shoulders, refastened the beautiful old brass fibula that held it. You're looking good—something does happen at thirty, and you're the sort it's becoming to. It's a good age, don't blow it. This is the end of the first year of your very own Five-Year Plan, and so far it's working. If you can just keep afloat.

A young seamstress from the large atelier next to Erica's workroom came in with a gauze tunic; she didn't quite understand collars, not surprising since Moroccan women didn't have them on their own clothes, which were all made by men anyway. What ghastly cloth, almost cheesecloth, and twice the price it was last year, too. "This way, Nejma—then reverse and doublestitch all around? Hmm?" The girl nodded shyly; she was coming along, but still wasn't very good on anything other than a straight seam, and ironing. Not to worry, though. The tunics were for what Erica thought of as the "Schlock Stock," no labels at all and sold at an enormous profit in one of the better tourist shops in the souk. No complaints and no returns, either. Not from Ostend or Antwerp or Trondheim, which is how far away they would be when first washed, and faded in streaks and self-destructed. The two girls she kept busy in the atelier cranked out the harem pants, caftans, tunics, flowing robes of no authenticity that the tour groups wanted. Erica had long ago come to terms with using the sleazy polyesters, fibranes, synthetics that were available, but even so the last forty meters of café au lait gauze she'd bought from that devil in Fès had been so slithery it'd been like trying to cut and sew aluminum foil to cellophane wrap.

And now that fiendish boutique in London, where she sent two collections every year of quality clothes made of what good wool and cotton she could find—those rotten bastards were trying to weasel out of paying the forty-five hundred pounds they owed her, and had owed for the last five months. They'd been very enthusiastic when they got them, Harper & Queen had given her things two full pages, and they'd virtually walked out of the shop by themselves, those clothes. Now the boutique was trying to base its payment on the export invoice prices, which was utter rot, as they knew. If she'd listed them realistically the export fee would have been prohibitive. They were suggesting five hundred pounds instead of forty-five hundred. Oh, Christ. Her best hope now was in the lawyer she'd been lent—thank heaven for generous friends—after going up there to tackle it herself last month, but the immediate problem was how to keep her head above water today and tomorrow. The old Hadj, bless his fuzzy old turban, would wait another month or two for the rent, but she had to pay "the troops," as she thought of the girls and Fats and SiMohammed, every week, feed them lunch and endless pots of sugary mint tea, the electricity, telephone. It'd be the end of the month before Driss reckoned up and paid her for what he'd sold in the souk, and with this weather her gauzy robes and ample caftans wouldn't appeal as much as his copper and leather and little inlaid tables; that was exactly where those big Nordic cows would plunk their guilders and kroner and marks and francs. Damn.

In the meantime, she was well into the rent Bettman had paid her this month for Gleb's house. She'd just have to count on old Gleb mooching around forever down south as he usually did, or not needing it immediately. She hadn't seen him when he was in town for the day yesterday, which was a good omen. Her 10 per cent commission for getting Arthur and the house together had gone in a day or two on back bills.

Oh dear. She went out to the balcony and looked down into the garden, where Debbysue was chatting with Fats. Arthur's friend looked a dismal prospect after all. Far too old to wear a pea jacket that had nothing to do with Yves, and her hair was either some colorist's Terrible Joke or just devil-may-care, practically patchwork. Wait, that brown and gray and beige jacket made from djellaba scraps had just the same colors, where the hell had she put it—

She was pulling it from deep in a wicker hamper to have one of the troops press it when she heard the door knocker again. Tossing it into the atelier, she ran to the window. Oh my God. A tiny woman in a spotless suede coat and boots and with a fortune of a handbag was coolly shaking hands with Debbysue. Neva! But not until

next week—? Oh hell. Still, this might be better after all.
She took the card from the kimono in the basket and
tossed it to the floor, tying up the little basket with a
length of her own special indigo and magenta floss that
was her "signature" and snipping off an extra long end.
Yes, very good indeed, no reason why Neva shouldn't
give Stanley a present, was there? She adjusted her mus-
tard silk cossack pants around her lean hips, smoothed her
hair, and with the basket under her arm ran down the
stairs to her luncheon party.

Stanley, Lord Overton, shook out his coat methodically
and draped it carefully over the back of an armchair to
dry. Outside, the rain-dotted swimming pool and dripping palms bore small resemblance to the fantasy of
travel posters. The lobby of the hotel had been planted
with disconsolate tourists, too full of heavy luncheons to
summon energy and find alternatives to going out, but too
determined to get their money's worth of the hotel to go
up to their rooms and sleep off the meal and the weather.
Two of the wicker tables in the new glass conservatory
were being used for bridge, uncomfortably because of
their lowness. Terrible mistake, the new decor, he
thought. The vast soft-sculpture lounges in the lobby
were particularly unfortunate, as if a giant Alsatian shep-
herd had wandered through and left his droppings behind—same shape, same color. A majority of travelers
prosperous enough to stay at the Mamounia were well
past the age when they had supple enough knees and
backs to do anything but fall awkwardly into the sofas,
and then writhingly and unbecomingly struggle up and
out. And plastic plants everywhere.

"Entrez." He had hardly heard the light tap on the
door through the sweater he was pulling over his head.
"That you, Digby? Half a mo." Stanley went back into his
bedroom and adjusted his ascot and collar, took his

glasses from his jacket pocket. "Did those cables get off, and have you had your lunch? I've got some things for you this afternoon."

The thin, sandy young man laid a small sheaf of letters on the coffee table and opened a leather folder. "Yes, sir, I went into the central P.T.T. and sent them off myself, and I had a sandwich in my room."

"Good. As for having things sent up to your room, fine, but if you want some drink you'll do better to help yourself from here." Overton waved to a row of bottles on a buffet by the balcony. "You've seen enough of my audits on the Canadian hotels to know what a fiddle bar bills are, and this place beats all. Two pounds for a beer. Scandal."

"Thank you, sir, I'll remember that."

"Might as well get some good out of the drink we did bring with us." There was a note of irritation in Overton's voice. "You'll have to put some sort of tag or disk on the traveling file when it gets here—never occurred to me the bar case looked so much like the other you'd confuse them and bring the wrong one as carry-on. Any word from the airline?"

"Yes, they think the file case may come in on this afternoon's flight. I'm to telephone the airport at five."

"Let's hope for the best, then. Now, let's see, what have we here? You've been busy." He picked up the clutch of letters and peered at them through his glasses in the thin light from the balcony windows.

"May I just step into your room and see if the valet has brought back your things?"

"What? Oh, yes. But next time see if you can't steam things out over the bath, will you? This is probably the only hotel in town with enough hot water to do it, no point not taking advantage of it. Ah, I see you got them to exchange the car—good lad. What'd they give us? A Mercedes? Good." He shuffled the blue form to the bottom of the pile. "I'll have to bring down something of my own and leave it here if all this with Jouti goes through.

"Here now, what's this? No, no, no. You'll have to talk to that man at the desk downstairs, they're not to charge the full rate for this suite until Lady O. arrives and takes the second bedroom, that was agreed. Rascals. Oh, by the way, send a note to the Vice Admiral suggesting I come by day after tomorrow, about ten or eleven, for a cuppa. That's the first day of L'Aid, nothing else going on. Amazing he's still alive. And see he gets an invitation to the do at the Center. Blind as a bat and gaga, but it'll make him feel good. Did the papers pick up the press release?"

"Yes, both *L'Opinion* and *Maroc Soir*."

"Good-oh, read me out a bit, will you, while I sign these."

" 'British Entrepreneur to Present "Lost" Churchill Painting to Garrison Center in Marrakech. Lord Stanley Overton, wartime aide to the great Winston Churchill and Chairman of the Board of Overton Enterprises, will present a supposedly lost oil sketch of the Koutoubia mosque painted in Marrakech in 1943 by the late Prime Minister of England to the Garrison Center. Lord Overton is a director of the Garrison Trust, a foundation with centers around the world for crippled children. The Marrakech center celebrates its tenth anniversary this year; Lord Overton said it seemed fitting that the painting, a view of the Koutoubia with the buildings that are now the Center in the foreground, be given a home in a city Sir Winston loved so much. The valise'—oh dear, we said footlocker, bad translating—'in which the painting had been stored was only just discovered during recent renovations at the Mamounia where the Overtons are frequent guests. Lord Overton said he had forgotten entirely that he had left it there when he returned to Casablanca with Sir Winston in 1943. Lord Overton was subsequently a prisoner of war in Sidi Ifni and had assumed the painting was among his things that were lost when his aircraft crashed in the Atlantic.' "

"Rather good, rather good. By the way, Digby, your French is very fluent. That from that Swiss thing you got onto?"

"Yes, sir. I feel quite rusty, actually. That's an excellent summer program, it gave me a fine head start at university. I hope it'll keep on going; fifteen is a very trying age for boys."

"Ha. At that age I was a grocer's lad, coal hauler, odd jobs for widows, lawns, hedges, furnaces, gutters, you know the sort of thing. No programs like that before the war, Dig. Yes, I've gotten that thing quite well endowed and there are some good people in the administration, it'll be ongoing. I would have liked a leg up in the law, myself . . . couldn't be done, of course, but I would have liked to have ended up on the bench. Ah, well."

"Excuse me, sir. Hallo, hallo? *Ah, oui, attendez un moment, s'il vous plaît, ne coupez pas.* London, sir."

"Overton. Oh, Brossy, yes, yes, yes. I thought I'd take a load off your mind about the Center here. Nipped in this morning and all's well. The American girl is holding the fort until that replacement gets here; I know she says she's leaving weekly, but there seems no particular rush. No, no, you know I'm delighted to look in when I'm down here. All going well, the housekeeper and SiOmar fill in the gap when Miss Kemp isn't around. Yes, young Abdellatif has taken over part of the teaching, French and maths, and does the accounts with Kemp. I'll be sending up the full report after I've seen the hospital and the doctors, just wanted to say there doesn't seem any need to rush anyone down from London, all's well. Right-oh. Yes, pouring here too. Good-bye.

"Now, Dig, have you the location schedule for that film crew? Let's see—ah, yes, here we are, they're in Taroudannt now. I want you to ring up Wranklin in London, at

that new agency of ours, Aurora or something like that—
have him get hold of that film fellow we hired, today, and
tell him to work with me directly from now on. Then get
a call through to what's-his-name in Taroudannt and have
him up here tomorrow morning, I'll see him at eleven.
The snake charmer's all wrong, for one thing, but let me
spread the gloom when he gets here. The main job is fine,
but there are just one or two things I can help with.
Damn that missing case, the photograms I brought from
London are in it.

"Now, the list for the do at the Center—bloody lot of
Poles in town, aren't there? Fronts for the Russians, of
course. Oh, yes, all the countesses, bless their little hearts,
and all the Ministers; no, we'll not have him, I really *can't*
stick a decorator who shows up in velvet knickers and an
Eton jacket and wearing riding boots—take him off. Dr.
Ladislav, the Princess, the Director here of course—I
think Raffeto's going to be here to see about making a
film. Keep an eye on the desk downstairs and get them to
tell you who else is around. There are one or two bankers
—well, we've time, that file will be along soon. Now, you
can get on with those other things while I put some ideas
from that lunch today with Jouti and his cohorts on a tape
for you. Oh, and do me a line to Bettman, tell him I'm
bringing that film chap along for dinner tomorrow. And
make out a check to Erica Portland on my account here
for five thousand dirhams, she's finding some things for
Lady O.'s birthday for me, can't expect her to work on
tick. Send that over by messenger right away. And I'll
need to see to those new leases on the King's Road prop-
erties the minute the file shows up. I've a new tenant in
mind. Well, let's get at it; perhaps we can get some tennis
in tomorrow morning if this blows over. Came down here
for a holiday, after all, didn't we?"

"Yes, sir, I believe we did."

Digby opened the door to the corridor and pulled himself back quickly. An exquisite tiny woman in suede with a perfection of bimetallic hair stood with a gloved hand raised to knock, a mass of luggage beside her in the charge of theatrically uniformed porters. Stanley looked up, pulled off his glasses, and dropped the tape he was about to insert into the recorder.

"Neva!"

"Hallo, darling. And Digby. Don't look as if I were a ghost—it was simply too depressing at home, isn't it silly. Absolute stair rods for days and there wasn't a thing I could do about Aunt Sarah's things after all, so here I am! I stopped by just before luncheon and asked them to tell you I'd be at Erica's, and to bring my things up, but of course they didn't."

"Splendid, splendid. Awfully dull so far, as you can see —but now that you're here the sun'll come out. A good flight?"

"Goodish. You know how I hate it. I saw you in the dining room deep in machinations with all those business-men of yours."

"Why didn't you come in? Jouti was there, he adores you."

"Darling, you were so much the businessman yourself, work was written all over the table—and your face, I might add. I lunched at Erica's, your little girl from the Center was there, a charmer. Erica looks a bit—harassed, I thought. And she said she'd been up to London last month; funny she didn't call me."

"Oh, she must have dozens of young people her own age to see, even when she's there for longer than over-night." Stanley was putting the recording machine into its case; it jammed slightly.

"Overnight? Oh, I see."

"Did you look at clothes?" He turned around and brushed his hands off.

"Not yet. There was an American woman there in extremis, poor thing. The airline lost all her luggage, and she's dressed in—well, what can only be called mistakes at best. But I'll go back tomorrow morning, perhaps. Meanwhile, my love, look what I found for you—I didn't know Erica was doing men's things, but I must say it's too lovely." The maroon kimono felt like warm cream in their hands as she gave him a light kiss on the chin. "What's on the book, anything amusing?"

"Oh, this and that, Digby'll bring you a list. I think we might run down south in a few days—I feel an urge to replay my early days in advertising; we've got a crew shooting some soap commercials, it'll be fun. Thank you, love, this is quite quite special. Huge pockets, too. Oh, dinner with Arthur Bettman tomorrow, you'll like that of course. He's convalescing from hepatitis, but I think he'll be up to going out to look at our land in the Palmerie soon. Now, if you want to have a lie-down while I finish up these things, we'll dine in Gueliz. New restaurant, La Trattoria." He looked almost Japanese, with his dark sideburns and moustache, wrapped in the kimono.

"Lovely. Yes, I'll see to my things and rest a bit. Darling, if we do build here are you really sure you won't miss Barbados? My garden there—"

"Oh, we shan't sell that, not by a long chalk. I should think the Grahams would lease it like a shot. God knows they're there all the time anyway. They'll look after your garden, darling. And I'll look after you."

"No word from the airport about my bags, alas." Helen, dumping baskets and parcels on the floor, flung herself exhausted on a chair facing Arthur's bed. "Bad news as far as my affection for flannel nightgowns and my old bedroom slippers go, but what the hell, I've found an entirely new way of life. What a designer your Erica is! Aren't these things wonderful? We rushed on into Gueliz afterward and nabbed the boots to perfect the look." She rotated an ankle, showing black kidskin into which were tucked full gray flannel pants, the jacket that matched her hair lined in flaming red silk, a shoulder bag rich in braid work sewn on neat wool. "No buttons, no zippers, lots of pockets, elastic waistbands! I ordered myself blind, you can't get me away from here for weeks. That girl's got a future."

"Indeed she does. I wouldn't be averse to backing part of such a venture, but she'd have to get out of here first. Too many problems, not enough clients."

"It must be maddening. Well, lunch was just fine—I'll spare your liver and not recount the eats, but they were bliss."

"Speaking of menus, I hope you found something to wear tomorrow night?"

"Oh, the Overton thing. Yes, I have some clean rompers and ruffled socks, don't worry. You'd better set another place, though. Lady Overton has arrived." Helen reached over to the bedside table and poured herself a glass of tea.

"Neva? She wasn't expected till next week. A pity—"

"If that makes too many, I can go out, you know, or have a tray."

"No you don't. You're to talk to her while I talk to the men. Or listen to them, which is more my style. What brought Neva down betimes?"

"Winter, I should think. And some business she was trying to cope with that was being held up—she didn't quite say. My, she's very—perfect, isn't she? An ounce or inch or carat or dollop of anything and she'd be all wrong. She's like a museum piece, don't you think? What's he like?"

"Stanley? All right, lots of vigor, sideburns, moustache, Italian tailor, all that. Very much the self-made man, not what *I'd* call a ravishment to the eye anymore—fifty-eight —but a great deal of presence. You'll like him. Has an oar in an appalling number of things financially. Good works as well, of course. The peerage was earned, I must say."

"Lady O. seems to the manner born. She seemed a bit piqued Erica hadn't paid court or called or something when she was in London last month. Well, perhaps not, it was just a passing moment. The most important problem at lunch seemed to be Debbysue's departure. The kid's been at it for three or four months now and seems to get as far as the Casablanca airport and changes her mind. Thinks of yet one more souvenir or present to buy, or country souk to visit, or friend in some mountain hamlet to see. It must be hard after four years—that's a long time at twenty-six to have lived someplace. Especially when where you're going is Shreveport."

"And when you're leaving behind one of the most gorgeous men—as you'll see tomorrow. But don't fool yourself, that girl may be having a vacation now, but in the long run she'll get back to Louisiana and end up governor of the state in everything but name. She'll marry an heir to something and push and wheedle him into living out her ambitions. I can predict all this, you see, by the way she gives me my injections."

"Oh?"

"Yes. With SiOmar it's something like a sexy mosquito bite, but with little Miss Kemp, you never feel a thing. Slips it in so painlessly you don't know it's happened. She'll do the same thing with Mr. Whosis. Her head will always rule her heart, that one."

"Lucky girl, then. I liked her a lot, you know."

"Oh, so do I; organized emotions are always attractive, no mess. Well, any gossip about projects? Your ear was to the ground, I hope."

"Alas, not a word. Except that Neva, who quite likes you, sends her best. Speaking of best, did you know Erica makes things for men?"

"No, she doesn't. Or does she? Has she been holding out on me?"

"Oh, she had a heavenly . . . well—Moroccan-Japanese kimono sort of thing, you'd have loved it, but Neva nabbed it right off for Stanley. As a matter of fact I think Erica had been going to give it to him herself—"

"Never. I cannot conceive of Erica giving away anything she could sell."

"Sell, then. While I was wallowing in her couture upstairs after lunch an earring came off and I had to scrounge around the floor to find the doohickey that goes on the back; there was a note under her table to Stanley about it."

"So. Well, as long as she's paid for it, and I assure you she will be, I doubt she cares. She's on to a good thing there, he's planning an extravaganza of Maroc-iana for Neva's birthday this month. Well, dashing as your getup is, I wish it inspired me to don more than another of landlord's ratty old djellabas. Oh, God, I am so tired all the time that my *hair* hurts."

"Give in to it, old shoe." She began tidying the books on the floor, set the tea tray outside the door, took the jewelry he had been examining with a magnifying glass from the blankets and put it in a leather box on the table. "Hey, that's not my *Times*, is it? Damn you, Arthur, if you've been at my puzzle . . ."

"No, no, just looking up Overton Enterprise shares. Puzzles—if you're desperate Kauder has some old *Times*es around the house, you needn't fear cold turkey."

"All right. Any aches you want rubbed or brows you want sponged?"

Arthur's only answer was to groan and burrow farther into his bed, leaving visible only one languid yellow hand.

CHAPTER III

Debbysue Kemp lay in a snuggle of love, the cheap acrylic blankets and coarse sheets pulled up around her, listening to Mustapha Jouti splashing vigorously in the bathroom. Why, for heaven's sake, did Moroccan men have to leap up from bed like they were crawling with unspeakable germs the minute they'd finished making love? From what her girl friends told her with giggles, it was absolutely typical of men here, something that went with the territory. An awful bore. Such a darling man, though.

The gold filigree belt he'd brought her today—one of the traditional gifts of groom to bride, although they'd both avoided that connotation easily—must have cost almost a thousand dollars. Jeepers. And really good caftans like the one he'd given her three months ago when she'd almost left were at least half that. Nothing stingy about him, but if she didn't go home for sure this time he'd run out of things, the old sweetie.

He was a sweetie, even if he did keep her tucked away hole-in-the-corner. Heaven knows, she had to do the same thing—anything that went on at the Center everybody from the hot-water man and the beggars outside by the Koutoubia, down to the smallest boy inside, knew about right away, and living there she couldn't exactly flaunt him around either. Fair's fair. And he was just too noticeable around town, and around the country too, as well as too status-conscious on top of it, to be flashing a little nobody Peace Corps girl around the hot spots. Movie stars and fashion people were his style, and Russian "phosphate experts"—which stood for oil, of course, they'd never give up on that dream in the Sahara—and German businessmen were his world.

That youngest sister of his was due to marry pretty soon now—he'd gotten it all arranged with a friend of his. The older girl, with the bad squint, would get to stay home with Mama, then, like a lady in waiting to her and to his own wife when he married. Which he'd better get busy doing pretty soon. He wanted lots of kids, of course; no matter how modern he thought he was, there was a young girl around somewhere who would end up in his chilly high-walled villa and never go out except to the baths, or a ladies' afternoon party, or an ear-piercing for a little girl, and always wear a djellaba and veil instead of the jeans she might be prancing around in now, trying to kid herself she wouldn't have eight gold teeth and a kid for each one by the time she was forty. Come to think of it, she yawned to herself, I don't think I've ever seen a pregnant gal anywhere here who didn't wear a djellaba or a haik. And, with the first baby tied on her back and the second one on the way, up went the veil and hood— forever.

He'd put off marrying for a little bit, maybe; she'd seen him looking hard at Erica more than once. She burrowed her head uneasily into the bolster; it wasn't jealousy so much as a feeling that Erica might not be—well, nice to him. She'd be irresistible, of course, with those looks, and she sure could hold her own with anybody socially. Why was it Jouti and all his rich Moroccan buddies thought it was tacky for foreigners like herself to speak really good Arabic, but not French? Well, Erica spoke both darn well, so no problem there.

He came out of the bathroom half dressed and began pulling on his shirt. "Excuse me a moment, little one, I must see the *guardien* and give him his *cadeau* for L'Aid."

That horrible old man who looked after Jouti's precious
olive trees and was always hanging around this little
house in the middle of the grove. Oh, well, it was by far
the nicest place they'd had to be together in, as well as
the handiest; not far out of town and she could get here
easily on her little Moped. All those awful grubby hotel
rooms in dreary places—Ben Guerir and Beni Mellal and
Safi. Nice souks there, though—too bad he didn't enjoy
them at all. Erica'd get the big hotels, Rabat, Fès, Essaouira, el Jadida. Besides having her own house right
here, with some privacy. But I just don't see her with him
—he does want to be adored, and she's kind of like the Ice
or Snow Queen, the one with the splinter of ice in her
heart. Still, if I don't get out of here for good they'll both
die of old age, he's too much of a gent to do anything till
I'm gone. I'd love to catch that souk at Tiznit on Wednesday, it's the only place in the whole country they have
those green clay butter churns . . . but how'd I get it
home—

What a scene it's going to be back in Shreveport—all
my old chums married and with kids and covered in Spanish moss, likely. Still, if I do want to find Mr. Marvelous, it
won't be here, it's time to go—

"Time to go, little one." He bent over and kissed the
back of her neck. She looked up and into his dark, handsome face, so familiar, but the man himself forever
strange and never to be fully perceived. I love him so,
how fragile he is, she thought simultaneously. All sorts of
terrible things could happen—that war down in the desert
could get to be like the one in Algeria, with bombs tossed
into cafés—kidnappings—there could be another coup
against the King, too, that was always in the air. He could
die without ever knowing he loves me as much as he'll
ever love anyone. He wouldn't believe it even if his own
mother told him, but it's true, he does. He'll love his
bride, of course, but no more and no less than he loves me.

That's sad, too—guys here are sort of stunted in that area. Love has to have some respect in it, and this is sure no place for a woman to get that.

"Yes, honey, time to go."

"Now, you must not be *désolée*, my sweet, but if it is truly tomorrow you leave I will have to have one of the gardeners drive you to Casablanca. It is most tiresome, but of course I must spend L'Aid with my family, and perhaps late in the afternoon see Overton, then go to Rabat to see the Polish chemists any day."

"Oh, honey, I'd planned on taking the bus anyway, I've already got my ticket. Six in the morning."

"But that is *terrible*—those buses, they are for the *farmers!*"

"You're so cute, I got to Marrakech on a bus four years ago and it'll be fun to leave the same way—besides, I like your farmers."

"As you say," he shrugged, handing her her dress. "Now are you quite sure you have your seat on the airplane, that your ticket is in order?"

"Yessir, yessir. I'll spend tomorrow with my girl friends in Casa and be on the early flight the day after. Well, I'm ready—bye-bye, little house, olive grove—time to go, time to go. Come on, honey, you'll want to change for Arthur's dinner party and it's dark already. Time to go."

"Where else would he be but *le grand sud?* Tan-Tan or one of those places with too many *t*'s. You know Gleb, Jouti—he could be mooching around his beloved desert and never notice if the sky fell in. Actually he's no farther than Taroudannt right now, earning a packet with a film crew as translator and so on. I expect he'll ring me up at some point—any message?" Erica handed a martini to Jouti and a vodka to Helen.

"So very kind, Erica. Just that I would like to see him when he returns. But a dilemma, for that will not be until his house is empty and there will be no more of this lovely Helen and my good friend Arthur. Insupportable! You have just arrived, madame? So good for Arthur to have a friend, a boring disease—we have all had it one time or another, but it is not fair to visitors. You must let me arrange for you to see anything you wish, entertainments, museum, countryside—" He drew Helen toward the fireplace, resolved to acquit himself of his social duties to this unknown quantity before Overton arrived. Lady Overton was fond of attention, and that left him only the time after dinner for some serious progress with Bettman and Stanley. Bullock—he should have had his office in Rabat find out about her, it sounded familiar, could she be important?

Yes, it was likely a good thing Bettman was staying in Gleb Kauder's house; when the time came he would have some firsthand experience of the problems, on top of the perspective of having stayed at the Mamounia often. He would know what was needed to compete— It would all have to wait until Overton had become a bit more realistic, accepted the fact that without Jouti he could do nothing about all the other hotels. They were both keen on the project, there was no reason it wouldn't work out; Overton was fair, just. Time, however. And no one must have a hint of this project of his own, not yet, or the Englishman would want a part of it as well. He'd have to be satisfied with the others, the great *ksar* at Tifletoute, the Todra gorge, something inventive at Tata—what these crazy Europeans saw in the desert was a mystery, but they saw it. The work, the "arrangements" in Rabat would be difficult; the old families, the banks, the other Ministers—only he himself could do that, of course. Overton had panache, though, this little flower in Marrakech's buttonhole of the Churchill painting didn't hurt a thing and made both of them look quite . . . benevolent, philanthropic, and so forth. Let Khayat have that grazing land they'd pinched from the Tounfit herders for an "agricultural experiment station"—the south was where the money was for himself.

"Yes, there are many tour buses now, are there not?" he responded automatically to this woman's questions, "but independent travelers there are as well, the summer is becoming the season for the young. The beaches, fishing, scuba, climbing, the mountains, and, as always with the insane English, the desert. How I do love them, the English, so cool, fair, so—cerebral."

"It's a wonder they don't burn to a crisp." Erica stood beside them. "I do. But you know, Jouti, they are so like your own women, the English girls. Their men are still the peacocks too—one so often sees a strapping lad or two sitting in a camper while the girls change the tires, fill the water bidons, all that." She filled his martini glass from a pitcher, offered Helen lavender-colored olives. "I find it amusing, of course, particularly when their beaux get a glimpse of your young boys. The girls are instantly stranded at *le camping* and the van gets a good thorough clean while *their* lads are out on the tiles with *your* lads. Very English, that."

"Ah, not so, that is only Tanger with the old schoolmasters flying down for their weekends with the trash up there—it is too cruel of you to count Tanger as typical of this country yet, Erica. It will take much time to erase those European vices up there."

"Difficult to do and keep the foreign currency coming in at the same rate, I'd think. Your drink, Helen?"

"In a second, thanks. I'm feeling human for the first time in days. I was on the roof all afternoon in the sun—what a view of the mountains! I felt like a Baked Alaska, hot sun and cold snow. And interesting, all the ladies doing the laundry and wool hanging out to dry and so forth. Your restaurant, Dar Toubkal, it's really quite close, you don't realize from the street. Then this dress to keep all the warmth in my bones. Lovely wool, Erica."

"Isn't it? One of the two good cloths in the whole country. I call it 'couscous' because of the little nubs."

"But charming!" Jouti said. "In Arabic it is less attractive—pimple cloth. I took a djellaba made from it to Oxford my first year, not knowing about your English soots. It was not this creamy white that suits you *so* well, Helen, for very long."

No wonder Debbysue had been having lead feet about leaving, Helen thought as she went over to the little bar on the windowsill. He's so gorgeous, so glossy—as if his mother had given birth to a plump prune instead of a baby, and then soaked it in warm almond milk until manhood. And charming. She felt as if she had been used like a set of Indian clubs in his social gymnastics, to keep his line supple by limbering up on whatever was at hand until the main event. Which might very well be Erica—his attention had been entirely on the younger and cooler presence beside Arthur, her silk bell of hair revealing and concealing the milk-sherbet skin, the long, frail hands helpless-seeming with a weight of silver rings.

"You're not sick, are you? I don't see a sign of a drool." Arthur stumped out a cigarette and pushed another pillow behind his back.

"No, feeling fine, and no drool, no. He's a bit too fond of himself, to say nothing of being a bit young, for me at least."

"You're too choosy, always were. Let me tell you, Helen, you can't afford it anymore, not at our age."

"No? It seems to me I can't afford not to be. Having enjoyed the very best, I don't feel either obliged or panicky to settle for less." She grinned at him and ate an olive.

"Less? Hardly call him that—great big stud. And a very powerful force here to boot, has his tentacles into everything. He and Overton—it'll be amusing to see who eats whom alive before their shenanigans are over. What time is it, they're late."

"Not really. Have an olive. No, better not. Tonic?"

"Put some lemon in it. Oh, don't make a pig of yourself tonight, that thing is on for tomorrow morning. SiOmar's expecting you at eight-thirty sharp."

"That's a terrible hour. In the *morning?*"

"Are you going to the Center for L'Aid?" Erica and Jouti joined them. "I'd have asked you to my house, but there's nothing doing, the servants like to go to their own families and I adore having the place to myself for once. I'm going to spend the day soaking my elbows in grape-fruit or something equally cosmetic. You'll enjoy it, though, quite a show, and if you feel noddy there's always a long, boring gap between the slaughter and the meal. Run up to Debbysue's old room and have a nap. She sent fond farewells to all, by the way—I'm putting her on the bus at the crack of dawn." Erica pushed her long angel sleeves up her slim forearms. "This must be the Overtons. Come along, Helen, let's haul the corpse upright for the guests of honor."

"Hello, hello—Arthur, you're losing all that yellow, heard you were a veritable saffron, but I don't see it. Hallo, Jouti, Neva's been looking forward to seeing you again. Erica, my dear, salutes from your two most fervent admirers. You'll be Helen Bullock, of course, delighted, liked your work for years." Stanley led Neva into the room; a burly silhouette closed the doors behind them. "Very good of you, Arthur, to let me bring my colleague along—had to get him up from Taroudannt to straighten a few things out, and now we find it's worse than we thought. Your friend Gleb, Erica, apparently he's done a bunk, gone off and left the film crew without a translator and so on. All the more reason for this young man to meet you. May I present Fergus Bede?"

"And so the old chicken house is gone forever. What a mercy. I may dare show my face there again now that I don't have to cope with hot mash for those damn birds. Terrible tyrants."

"Oh, yes, all gone, and lots of nice new paint on the house itself and a new bathroom and the floors scraped and so on. Simon's full of plans for a garden where the chicky birds were. I think you'll like it all."

"And how's the old dad? Keeping an eye on Penner, I hope. That man's a terror on the costs."

"I don't really know, Simon was in Edinburgh when I left—half something at the Cathedral and half something with your godmother, the last I heard. I sent him a postcard from Heathrow telling him he'd better get back to his thatch. I knew you were working somewhere in the sun, but I don't think Simon said it was here. But how nice it is. How's it going?"

"Don't ask." In Fergus's large hand the snifter of cognac looked like a doll's thimble; he drank it down as if it were necessary to his survival. "Sorry—do ask, of course. But not me. Until yesterday I thought it was going well; now Overton, who saw the rushes in London, has put his oar in and I fear for the worst, especially with Gleb Kauder walking out this morning. I was counting on him particularly for this last bit—one sixty-second commercial, and we'd found a bit of blasted heath that would serve for the desert just outside Taroudannt, and rounded up some camels and so forth and fake blue men of sorts, all Kauder's specialty. Now Overton's decided it must be authentic, real blue men, real desert. Funny about Kauder— he just left a message at my hotel he wouldn't be back, family reasons, I think."

"Family? I thought he was a loner, somehow—"

"I too, I probably misunderstood the desk clerk. The French accent here is a bit confusing to me—singsong, isn't it? Well, I daresay the Centre Cinématographique in Rabat will send someone down."

"What are these commercials for? Television, I know, but what's being sold?"

"Soap, dear Helen, good old soap. Called, for the moment, Zippy. It's a combination of detergent, deodorizer, bleach, latherer, lotion, scourer—the line is 'it's so good it cleans everything but blackmail' and the scripts, very soft sell, call for all the dirty jobs in the world being rendered pure as snow. We've done Greek olive pressers, Italian grape crushers, Japanese fish factory, English blacksmith, Saudi oil rigger, sponge divers, chocolate factory, Channel swimmer covered with grease, Indian snake charmer—the lotion effect for the scales, you see—the list is endless. The blue men are to be the last, praise be. A bit esoteric, some of them—I imagine only about six will be used in the end."

"Bring me up to date on them, the blue men. I forget."

"Oh, those nomadic chaps down by Goulimine and on into the Sahara. Turbans and robes of indigo cotton, the dye comes off on the skin and they have somewhat cyanotic blue faces and hands."

"Yes, I remember now. How does Stanley fit into this? You say he's joining you—is he into soap on top of everything else?"

"I wouldn't doubt it. I do know the ad agency that hired me and mine is one of his many minor subsidiaries. A finger in all pies even now. He got all fired up looking at those rushes in London and decided to contribute his enthusiasm and knowledge of this country to the project, damnit. 'As long as he was going to be here on holiday anyway.' Someday I will be given a job to do somewhere that no one in the world would care to join to rip off a holiday fiddle. This happens all too often—it's a terrible waste of time."

"Keeps you from burning with a hard, gemlike flame, hmm?"

"Ouch. But in point of fact, commercial though I am and this work may be, there is a fine thread woven throughout of the Bede touch, old girl, and it's that genius of mine that's going to pay off one day and keep the

Aging P. and you in wheelchairs and gin, so don't shoot me down."

"Hmm. I hadn't, somehow, thought ahead to spending my declining years rocking on the porch at Crumbles. Interesting thought. If that's to happen you'd better have Penner get to work—the old porch was full of rot and Simon had it carted away with the chicken house."

"Just as well. It wasn't big enough for two." His eyes, a darker hazel than Helen's, were set and shaped exactly like Simon's blue ones, and she enjoyed that familiar warm twinkle in them, even though the rough dark hair and eyebrows were the young man's own and owed nothing to anyone she knew about. Helen wondered if some legendary Welsh giant figured in the family background; Fergus was easily six-three or -four. Were it not for the inborn relaxation and warmth he had inherited from Simon he would almost glower.

"So many things seem to be filmed here; is it cheaper, or what?"

"Yes, there's that. Also, climate, geography, good weather insurance rates, and a super place to fake things in, you see. So many physical types, you can have a crowd of 'American Indians' or 'Greeks' or whatever just by costuming, and there are plenty of foreigners living on beans—students, missionaries, whatever—they love to fill in. Seacoast, too, caves, grottoes, waterfalls—all within a day or two from each other."

"Is this the sort of thing Jouti is involved in, Developing and Liaising?"

"Oh, quite small beer for him personally, he'd only be involved in Lawrence of Arabia—that film center in Rabat might be under his ministry, I don't know."

"Speaking of dirty jobs, have you a mahout washing down a white elephant?"

"My God, no, and don't mention it. I doubt there's one

in the whole country—Hannibal must have nabbed the last."

Across the room Arthur had given up expending his waning energy on sitting upright between Jouti and Stanley, and was lounging back on the banquette watching with one languid eye as Erica and Neva played backgammon. The other eye, Helen knew, was not only watching, but was in company with his two ears in absorbing every nuance of the conversation; the cadence and dynamics were audible enough so that even without hearing their words Helen could tell it was still parry and lunge, lunge and parry time. Maddening for Arthur, who was only interested in a specific that would or would not involve him.

"Fergus, kid, I think I'd better break this up and put Arthur out of his misery, he's about to get fretful. Can you come to the slaughter with me in the morning?"

"Alas, Overton's sending me out to a place called Oum Nast to look at a Berber *ksar*—a background for what I can't imagine, but he's the boss. I'll call you when I get back in the afternoon."

"Great. Arthur, you're up too late, Dr. Riad would not approve. You'll all forgive me if I send him up to bed?"

"Of course, of course." Stanley rose absentmindedly as he replaced Helen's newspaper on a pile of periodicals that had been beside him on the banquette. "You must watch yourself, Arthur, careless of me— I say, d'you think you'd be up to a spin one day soon in the Palmerie to look at that land of mine—all this rain, I have a feeling it may need more drainage than it has."

"Good idea." Arthur began shaking hands. "Tomorrow afternoon? I'm looking forward to getting out and about. We should all see it together in any case. I've been thinking about the placement of the house, it's tricky."

"Splendid, we'll come for you at three. Neva, away from the gaming table. You've cleaned Erica out to begin with, I see, and I've worn Arthur out. Helen, I have an imperative for you, you must go along with the boys and SiOmar after the slaughter in the morning—I've gotten a little airplane organized to take all of you up for a spot of sightseeing, the mountains and all that. You'll be enchanted."

"What a nice thing for you to do—I'll love it."

"Don't look so grim, Erica darling." Neva was smiling, crushing a wad of banknotes down into her little evening bag, the diamonds on her fingers and the clasp glittering. "You're only a thousand dirhams down and it's all play money anyway—now I do want to see some clothes tomorrow, but be a duck and don't call me until one at least, Stanley has to totter off in the morning and see the old Vice Admiral, but I'm taking an enormous sleeping pill and shan't lift my head from the pillow until then."

Helen stood at the street door, waiting for Erica, who had gone upstairs with Arthur. She watched the others start down the street toward Dar Toubkal's one light on the corner, the dark archways beyond. They turned the corner, disappeared. Erica stepped over the sill, wrapped thoroughly in a long wool cape, brushed Helen's cheeks with "good night, good night" and hurried after them, her shadow wavering in the one lone light. A late householder stumped by in the other direction, a large, calm sheep slung over his shoulders just as one would bring home a Christmas tree. A cat, suddenly antic, streaked out of the shadows at Erica's feet. She stumbled, brushed for a moment against the sheep's hooves. Her cloak fell from a shoulder, and as she swirled it back in place Helen saw a drape of luminous cloth beneath, the glint of velvet, of gold thread. Which had nothing to do with the finely pleated black gown Erica was wearing.

CHAPTER IV

"Oh, lordy, here I go." Debbysue tipped the busman who had hauled an unbelievable number of baskets and bags onto the top of the bus, and turned for another hug from the tearful Lalla Kinza, who was almost invisible between the rhinestone sunglasses and her veil. The girl's own tears left a damp spot on the bosom of the woman's brown gabardine djellaba. She mopped at it with her handkerchief, laid her head for solace one last time on that vast warmth.

"Oh, it's so—gee, the souk buses I've gotten on here, all the good times—"

Erica shivered; this indeterminate morning darkness didn't evoke anything in her but an overweeningly strong desire to get back to bed, but then she wasn't leaving Marrakech this morning. Not just yet.

"No you don't, Deb, I've said 'good-bye' here once too often, you've got to go. Honestly, I think if Jouti had given you a gross of old men's djellabas instead of that gorgeous caftan you'd be happier, all those grotty things from the souks are what you like best."

"Oh, maybe, but don't you worry, this is it, I'm really going. You know, Erica, maybe you should be thinking about it too? It's been just a grand place for us for a while, but—"

"I know, for will-be's and has-beens. I've your address, and I'll see that SiOmar here gets your rugs to the post office."

"Darling of you to get up so early and come over,

Erica. You have a wonderful year, hear, and come see me at home if ever you can?"

Even with tears she was perky and plucky, Erica thought as, giving one last hug to SiOmar and Lalla Kinza, and a kiss to the young teacher Abdellatif on his crutches, Debbysue marched up the steps of the bus just in time to take a seat as it began to pull away from the station in Djemma el Fna.

Oh, my nice warm bed waiting, she thought, I'll refill my hot-water bottle and have a good lie-in until ten, at least. "Bye now, SiOmar, Abdellatif. Come on, Lalla Kinza, here's a calèche, I'll be going right by your house and drop you off."

Helen hunched inside her new jacket, her hands in the pockets still feeling the five small claws that had touched her before they kissed their own hands in respect. Now their little fists, hardened with leather working, weaving, thin and knuckly and powerful with compensating for the legs that had failed them, were propelling the boys on their little skateboards all about the courtyard. Abdellatif, with a shy welcome for Helen, his eyes bright with pleasure behind his heavy glasses, sat in a low, rusty wheelchair, adjusting a trickle of water from a hose. SiOmar, who had somehow managed a lengthy brush of his arm against Helen's bosom while showing her the fine largeness of the ram, was trussing the hind legs of the sheep together.

From somewhere outside and above a siren screamed for half a minute, then the hushed quiet of the holy day morning descended expectantly. "That is the signal that the King himself has sacrificed now at Rabat, and we may proceed!" Abdellatif hustled the short boys into a line by the pool, swatting and shouting exactly as if they were young lambs themselves, driving them back, laughing, to a somewhat serious line. The little pool was over half full now, fodder and straw and leaves floating on the surface, a plastic bottle cracked with age, tangerine peel.

SiOmar hauled the hobbled sheep from the corner, not seeming to feel the icy jet of water on his feet as the hooves gently kicked the dribbling hose. He held the sheep's head in one hand, straddling the body with his powerful legs like a clamp, and with a swift prayer called out "In the name of Allah" with his eyes closed. His hands stretched the head up, exposing the curly neck. He took the large knife Abdellatif was holding for him, and expertly slashed across the neck, through the thick wool and hide and muscle directly to the artery, which released a steaming thick jet of blood that pulsed and throbbed in a slowly, slowly decreasing arc.

A long, slow ooh and ahh from the boys, who were otherwise utterly quiet; Helen watched the sheep's eyes lose their brightness, glaze, and pale. SiOmar dropped the head and loosed the body, letting it fall on the tiles, the forehooves twitching delicately as the last of life pumped itself out in the vaporing stream traveling slowly across the chill tiles. How long it takes, she thought. Then the hooves were still.

The head was severed quickly and cleanly, tossed in a corner. With one arm SiOmar lifted the now quite literally dead weight of the body and straight-armed it above his head, flashing a smile at Helen, hooking the hobbled hind legs over a meat hook projecting from the wall. The boys erupted with excitement, rolling about with pans and basins and the hose as the skin was loosened around the flanks and peeled off as one would a sweater, clean and undamaged. Steam rose from the suddenly bare carcass, which without the head and woolly skin became just that: a carcass, hanging as if in a shop, so much meat for so many people. No longer awesome, but a commodity.

A slit down the belly and the intestines tumbled out, were grabbed and gathered in messy hilarity by three of the boys who stretched them out, like a fire hose for washing later, squeezed them from one end to the other, extruding undigested fodder that oddly enough was not unpleasant, only biological.

The little skateboards tracked blood over the courtyard as the liver, stomach, heart, kidneys were tossed to the boys for washing and soaking in their various basins. Somehow the holy moment seemed over; Helen lit a cigarette and turned to shield her lighter from the puffs of wind that were tearing the thin clouds apart. Standing by the open iron gate at her back was an extremely gray-flannel young man with a London haircut and polished shoes and a face so green his white lips looked more grotesque than pathetic.

"Here, have a puff on this, or put your head down or something."

"Thank you very much indeed," he managed, taking the cigarette and inhaling deeply. He dabbed his forehead with an impeccable handkerchief, breathed slowly, and began to look as if he would live. "I'm Digby Marshall, Lord Overton's secretary. Sorry, I just wasn't expecting—I've come to see about the boys' airplane ride."

"A real slaughterhouse, isn't it? I'm Helen Bullock, I met your boss last night. What a great treat he's giving the kids today, really nice."

"We hope so. The sky's clearing, it should be sunny."

The courtyard was increasingly hectic, slippery, bloody, and wet. SiOmar's head seemed to be inside the sheep's very body. He withdrew it and, smiling through the gore, advanced with a dripping hand. "*Sbah Lxir*, Sidi Marshall. *Labess?* A shame, you not here when sacrifice. You make good witness, good *bzef*. *Seulement* me for witness, I am man of house only. A shame."

"Ah, but I was here, wasn't I, SiOmar, from the beginning!"

"*Oui, belle Hélène*, but must to have two women, more

if can, for one man to be witness. Our women careless, forget, not understand what they see and hear, change her thoughts. They stupid and always many lies. Yes, we must to have two if they are women. But to come in drink tea now."

"Um, I think we'll run over to the Café de France, thanks, I need cigarettes and we'll get some coffee there, back in a minute."

It took all Helen's need for sugarless caffeine to get herself and Digby out of the gate before SiOmar could imprison them with a pot of mint syrup. Digby caught her elbow as she slipped on a stone and brushed against the Center's little van parked outside. He blanched as she pulled herself up and she saw there was a streak of blood on the bodywork. "That horny little rascal—I thought my fancy footwork had paid off, but he did get another feel after all, with those gory paws. Poor thing. I'm wearing so many layers of clothes that if I didn't feel a thing he really couldn't have either."

"You know, it's as close to Christmas morning in feeling as I can think." Helen put down her coffee and waved her hand at the deserted sidewalk café and Djemma el Fna beyond, the great *place* empty of all save a cluster of raincoated and disappointed-looking tourists with useless cameras dangling from their necks. A lone calèche clopped emptily by; no radios blared, no horns honked. A butcher, his small assistant importantly carrying knives in a wooden bucket, followed a portly man in layers of fine woolen djellabas, his prayer rug folded neatly under his arm and an enormous bunch of mint in his hand. A rooster crowed in the distance, a sheep bleated; great patches of blue began to dominate the washy sky, which leaked more and more sunlight.

"Yes, that combination of calm and hope, isn't it. D'you know, the Moslems think we've got it all wrong in Genesis, that it was Ishmael Abraham offered as a sacrifice, not Isaac. Doing a bit of reading up last night. Now I wonder if Isaac were born then; it makes a difference, you see. After all, Ishmael was only a handmaiden's son, and if Abraham had Isaac to fall back on it does seem to make the intended sacrifice a bit less, doesn't it?"

"For Abraham, you bet your boots. Still, not so nice for the boy, whichever it was. Are you into Islam yourself?"

"No, no, just that recently I've had to do with something of a corollary, a parent who . . . perhaps not quite sacrificed, but certainly dedicated a son to God quite early in the boy's life, and I must say she meant it. In a positively medieval way. Might have gotten away with it too, if the boy hadn't died. What about another coffee, it's quite good?"

"Please. It must be interesting working for Overton; he seems into just about everything that'd be fun to know about."

"Indeed yes—very stimulating. I've only been with him this closely for a month, although I've been with the Enterprises itself for quite a time."

"Did he pluck you out of the troops himself for this job?"

"More or less, but he's always kept an eye on me. My father and he were prisoners of war together at one point; Dad was badly wounded, lived long enough to get home in '45, but I think pretty much straight to hospital. I was just a newborn then, of course, don't remember him at all, he died soon after. But Lord Overton—he wasn't a Lord then, of course—saw to it that everything was done for him that was possible, and looked after my mother's pension, all those things. He's been very helpful over the years. This, though, is almost dizzying at times."

Newborn just after the war? Helen did quick mental arithmetic. Yes, his looks were the indeterminate kind;

people like Digby aged in decades, not years. Thirty-five, something around there.

"And probably will be quite mundane at others, but you'll certainly get a look at how the world turns, if nothing else."

"If I last that long; my first delinquency was to take the traveling bar on board the flight and check the files with the other luggage. Now it's been lost."

"You too? I'm only waiting for my clothes—files are much worse. Don't fret, they'll turn up. Ask at the airport, if there's anyone there this morning. Well, I suppose it's time to amble back—the sky's all clear now, it'll be lovely."

"Yes, and there'll be two flights, by the way. The plane's a bit small, so that gives a bit of extra room; you can go up twice if you like."

"Oh, no, not even *once*. There are some things middle age lets one off the hook on, such as root canal work, for instance. I'm too old to suffer so much ever again, and affluent enough to afford bridgework if the need arises. One of the most definite things is riding in small planes. Also, nights in sleeping bags. Gin. Fiction in the *New Yorker*. False eyelashes. Japan. Jelly doughnuts. Paris. Anthony Tudor ballets. Navy blue anything. The list is endless. Small planes begin and end it, though."

"Oh, dear, dear. Lord Overton was so very pleased, he made quite a point of being sure you had the best seat and all that—it made up to him for Latif's not being able to go at all; the boy has an ear infection and the plane isn't pressurized."

"Poor kid. Well, just don't tell your boss I didn't go, let him get his vicarious pleasure. Now, that's a very enterprising guy—" Huddled outside the Koutoubia's door, an old man was stoking a fire under a rusty oil drum, selling tin cans of warm water to men for their ablutions before entering the mosque to pray. She stood by Abdellatif's wheelchair and waved good-bye as SiOmar tossed the boys into the back of the van like so many sacks of flour, admiring the genuine pleasure in the young teacher's heavily spectacled eyes as he watched his friends ride away.

Upstairs, Debbysue's room was a flurry of emptiness, abandoned baskets, discarded cartons, careless paperbacks and magazines. Helen rummaged through the room, collecting blankets and a pillow, and took them out onto the gallery looking over the grisly courtyard. Abdellatif was directing the little hose on the gorier spots, sweeping behind it with a rag. The pool was turning a murky pink; some of the color was from the sunshine reflecting off the rosy walls. Oh, lovely warmth and sun; Helen wrapped herself in the blankets, lay down on the gallery's banquette, and propped up her crossword puzzle, a bit grubby by now, on her knees. A short lion tamer follows sheep. 7. Oh, really. Nice up here. The open door at the opposite end of the gallery was lit with sun, dust motes were dancing over a desk littered with untidy files, open drawers. Lion tamer . . . she yawned, closed her eyes, and slept.

The rusty air conditioner in the wall by her bed was up to its old tricks again, making its usual horrid racket. She fumbled one hand toward the dials, and met instead a hard surface. Oh, God, *not* Twelfth Street with its big brass bed and dry electric blanket. Rain was clattering down again, pocking the roiling surface of the pool below, jumping like knife points off the tiles. Lalla Kinza was just running into the kitchen in her old brown gabardine djellaba and bare hennaed feet in plastic scuffs, a glint of the precious rhinestone sunglasses. Helen heard the door from the kitchen to the street slam, closed her eyes, and as she slipped back into sleep remembered . . . lion tamer, sheep, oh, of course, Ram a dan.

"—but then, dear Simon, the 'short boys' and SiOmar had their jollies, especially the airplane ride and the festive meal, before the sadness. That pool was so full of crud and filth and dust it was opaque, and although we all wondered what had happened to him I doubt anyone would have thought of looking into it if one of the littlest kids hadn't gotten absolutely centrifugal with too much party and too little rest and skidded in on his skateboard. We—SiOmar and I—pulled him out right away, but there was poor Latif at the bottom, with his crutches. A horrible bruise, more of a dent, on the side of his head; the police think he skidded in the rain, fell against the iron rail, knocked himself out and drowned. The ear infection could have made him dizzy, too—so many ways, the rubber tips on his crutches were worn and smooth as Teflon, for one thing, and he'd lost his glasses . . ."

Helen pushed the paper away and stood up for a moment, relieving the cramp in her back. The little she had understood, aside from her own observations, had been from a policeman; everyone else had shifted into Arabic immediately. He had politely taken her into the atelier out of the way from the tearful and shout-filled garden; she'd seen the broken eyeglasses herself as he talked to her, among the bits of wool, leather, string, orange peel on the floor under the looms. Picking them up, she'd untangled them from a length of dark floss tangled in the frames, handed them to the policeman, who had taken them gingerly. The heavy, bottle-thick lenses were broken into star crystals.

"Lalla Kinza was brought over, of course, but she swears on a pack of Korans she hadn't been there all day. I might have dreamed it, except that the hot-water man outside by the mosque had seen her too. However, nobody seems to think it's important. I suspect they all think she was pinching saffron or coffee or something—women are *expected* to steal, especially *servants*. Simon, it was such a sad and abrupt end to a gallant little life. I gather he wouldn't have lived a normal span in any event, he had TB of the bone on top of polio and enough other things wrong too, but it doesn't make this much better.

"D'you know what the saddest thing for me was? I mean, if I'd been working and had to photograph any of it, the thing that seemed the most telling and illustrative of Abdellatif's life were his crutches—his legs were so twisted and undergrown they weren't the crutches of an eighteen-year-old at all, they were a little boy's crutches, quite quite short."

CHAPTER V

"A Mauritanian *ear-wax* spoon? How distasteful." Arthur dropped the little object back into the bin of jewelry he was rummaging through in one of the "treasure rooms," as he thought of them. He had gone through the cupboards and was thwarting the cold by sitting on a sheepskin and wearing a turquoise felt robe that made his skin look even yellower than before. Erica laughed as the spoon found its place among broken Timex watches, cheap belt buckles, plastic amber, Woolworth costume jewelry. "How very versatile you are, Erica. So you're going off to fill in for my landlord with the film crew? Ah, well. I'll miss you, I hope you won't be down there long."

"I shouldn't think so—four or five days at the most. Stanley's paying me a packet, and I need a change anyway. Now, what can I do for you and yours"—she waved a hand toward Helen's room—"to see you're all right before I leave? No, no, that's not a belt, goose, it's a lady's headdress, not old but rather a good one, for weddings and things, it goes like this—bend down."

"And so the Overtons are going too— My God, how heavy this thing is." He peered in a hand mirror, the silver ornaments and coins and baubles on the thick felt bands weighing down his neck appreciably, covering his forehead, ears, the sides of his neck.

"Yes, Stanley's all enthused about it. A Zohra!" she leaned over the windowsill and called down, but there was no answer. "Blast. I want some coffee, be right back up." She loped down the stairs, passing Helen's still closed, shuttered window and door.

The elegant little quilted cotton jacket Erica had shed lay on a small cork stool by the window, the lining made up of strips of old silk neckties and piping the cuffs and collar. Ingenious, Arthur thought, she probably got them in an old clothes souk. Yes, there was reason to put an investment in Erica while she was up for grabs. Not only would the ever-turning wheel keep on revolving until elegance itself came up once more, but there was always a demand for casual clothes with style, the kind of clothes with classy sex and sexy class. Helen was an example— she'd looked unusually well put-together the other night, almost soignée except for that hair. Well, nothing to be done about *that*, never had been.

She'd never cared a hoot for fashion, Helen, but she'd always had style of a sort. The world's caught up to that now, and as she herself had said, in the last ten years clothes had gone from see-through to saw-through, what with punk shaved heads and barbed-wire jewelry.

Yes, Erica was a good thing; he'd have to find out what her plans were and what capital she could get her hands on—he never was a sole backer of anything, however promising. But she did have something up her sleeve; if he waited too long he'd do himself out of a piece of the action.

"You look like an emaciated version of Beardsley's Ali Baba." Helen draggled in, yawning, rubbing her head. "Dress-up time?"

"So you're finally up. Just as well." He pulled the clinking felt and silver bands from his head and passed the headdress to her. "Not really my style, but I must admit one would really feel quite married after wearing that at the ceremony. Erica's here, there'll be some coffee. She knows all about that boy yesterday, so *no* keening and moaning, you know I can't bear that sort of thing."

"Yes, I know." Helen fingered the silver, soft and dark and probably very impure, but some of the bits were charming, a bird, a turtle, odd shapes with bumps and knobs, strips of branch coral alongside red glass stones, a French telephone coin next to genuine coins, how droll. A round disk, not a coin, but with Roman lettering, she made out the letters PA ILC C of E. A British army identity disk, of course. She squinted into the sunlight. Was this next ivory, or bone?

"Helen, good morning." Erica stooped with the ritual cheek kisses, followed by Zohra with a tray.

"Now, Erica, you asked what you can do while you're away—the very best thing is to take Helen with you tomorrow, there's no reason for her not to see some of the countryside, and she can check in with me by telephone. If I have a relapse she can come back. She might be able to help that hulking young man, Fergus. After all, film's her métier. And cheerful news on postcards will be the best medicine for me just now. I trust my exasperating landlord isn't likely to pop up and want his house back now that he's not employed? I refuse to go back to that hotel."

"Gleb? Oh, no, there'd be no point really. After all, what could he do here now that it's all over? Besides, renting this is about his only income, you know, he lives on it. Had some Swiss ethnologists last year and stayed away for eight months. Hates towns and has cronies in the desert anyway. Helen, do you really want to come down with us then?" Now that what's all over, Helen wondered, still too sleepy to think. Erica was so fair she seemed almost transparent in the sunlight, her long fingers sorting piles of rings, bracelets on the rug she sat on. "Car space might be a problem—"

"Oh, she'll rent something and tootle along on her own, if anyone needs a lift there'll be room." Arthur came as close to a satisfied beam as he was able. "So there's no problem, is there? Are you a bit glum, Erica, or are you not?"

"Oh, not. No, of course no problem if Helen has a car, more fun that way for you anyway, Helen. Actually, I'm by way of cursing deaf heaven with my bootless cries this morning. Which is foolish, life is unfair and that's that, but Neva's inheriting almost one million quid is somehow rankling today. However, my bile doesn't really become me, she's a nice enough lady—the thing I begrudge is that it won't make any difference to her, really, she has more than enough already. I don't see Stanley keeping her on short commons, do you? Ah, well, perhaps there's some rich uncle in Australia I don't know about in my future."

"Perhaps, does no harm to hope. That's a very healthy sum for Neva, no matter what sort of pin money Stanley provides. Nice to know such large amounts can still be found, so difficult keeping one's capital together anymore. Your capital, Erica, however, is very likely your talent; you're a much downier bird, my girl. Is that mail, by the way, behind that coffeepot?"

"Oh, yes, sorry." Erica handed over an airmail letter and a postal card, which Arthur held up, an old black-and-white view of the Koutoubia minaret. "This one seems to be for you, Helen . . .

> 'There was a fair lady named Helen
> In a state of domestic rebellion
> Went off to Maroc
> Without a *barak-*
> *allaufik!* (I didn't mean to enfelon!)
>   S.'

Humph. Doesn't scan. *Baraka llaufik*, that's blessings or thank you or one of those you-Tarzan-me-Jane phrases. But enfelon? *Enfelon?* Nothing rhymes with Helen except melon."

"Humph to you." Helen smiled, taking the postcard from him. "Maddening he may be, but he's clever. Enfelon. It means to infuriate."

"That won't do. I refuse to travel like an Irish picnic. Those things'll simply have to go in the back seat with you, Erica, or down with Digby and Miss Bullock—she's sure to have room. I've always traveled like a gentlewoman and I don't intend to change. See to it, Digby. I'll be in the coffee shop when you've finished. Roof racks, indeed." Neva marched back into the lobby, leaving Erica to order the porters to unload the bundles and bags from the top of the Overtons' car and divide them between the back of the Mercedes and Helen's rented little Renault 4.

"Temper, temper," Erica murmured. "What's this all about, Digby? Did she have a bad night at the casino?"

"No, they're both a bit fagged, I think. Nervy. Himself's upstairs in a black fury because a suit's been lost. He was practicing his usual economy when he came back from the Vice Admiral's the morning of L'Aid, hung the suit he'd been wearing over the tub to steam the wrinkles out, but it fell in—had to give it to the valet, and of course they can't find it this morning. She had some sort of contretemps with a hairdresser yesterday—you know the sort of thing."

"Indeed I do. Crumpled rose petals in their path. Can this go in your boot, Helen?"

"It's full to bursting—oh, by the way, there's hope for you, Digby, I stopped by the airport after I picked up the car this morning, my bags are here! So, can yours be far behind? Take all the back seat, Erica, that'll be plenty of room. What, in heaven's name, if I may ask, *are* all those bales?"

"Blue. I don't trust the supply for a minute in Goulimine, especially with the guerrillas—all the cloth that used to come up from China via el Ayoun isn't anymore, and if you haven't learned by now you will soon that you can't count on anything in this country anyway. If I'm meant to see there are blue men, I'm going to be sure they're wearing the right kind of blue. This is some I brought up a year or so ago and hadn't made up into anything yet. A pity, Fergus could have taken it back down in his van yesterday. Digby, what in the name of the lord is this?"

Helen looked into the smart canvas fishing bag Erica was holding. More rhinestone sunglasses, printed T-shirts, costume jewelry, Timex watches, boxes of Pentel pens in many colors, inexpensive sweaters. "A Santa Claus bag?"

"Oh, more or less." Digby took it. "He said he always brings this sort of thing for presents—apparently they're very popular. I expect he'll want it with him, I'll put it under the front seat. Oh, dear, could this be one of her handkerchiefs?" He had pulled out a road map, a small ball of tea-colored cloth with embroidery.

"Let me just look at his road map, will you, we'll have to get our own on the way out of town, Dig." Helen spread it out on the hood of her car, noting mileages, place names. Some were circled, it was a bit worn along the folds, and a faint pencil had written on the Atlantic ocean "cheese, lotion, tobacco." A traveler's map. She gave it back to Digby, who put it back under the seat.

"Now," Erica said, "when you get to Goulimine you'll find the hotel right on the *place;* you'd do well to tell Fräulein Elfrieda you want rooms eighteen and nineteen for the Overtons—they're the only two with baths, and I'd like number fourteen upstairs as usual. She's a bit huffy and likes to think of herself as 'grand,' so a milord will be just the ticket, no doubt. We shouldn't be more than a day or so in Taroudannt—well, I suppose we might as well see if the car is suitable for her ladyship now. The cheese paring of the rich, paying a hundred pounds a

week for a Mercedes and yet quibbling at having a valet
press clothes. I ask you."

Helen awoke from a light doze as they left the outskirts
of shabbiness that declined from the upended dominoes
of Agadir's beach hotels, the clutter of Inezgane straggling away behind them into ambitious occasional false-
fronted cafés, closed now in despair and eroding to instant ruins, their bits of Day-Glo paint with wondrous
designs on the stucco proclaiming long-abandoned hopes
for prosperity. The sky was summer white, full of blown
dust. No djellabas on the women walking quickly along
the roadside now, but graceful haiks instead, the saris of
the south. Black, black against the bleached and stunted
earth, meters of cloth wound around, freely swaddling
and soothing, giving a glimpse of forearm, silver ring,
anklet, bronzed cheekbone, an end held in blazing teeth
against the face-revealing wind.

"Whatever it is that made your bossman so eager to be
authentic and haul Fergus down to Goulimine, I'm the
winner." Helen yawned and laid her head back on the hot
seatcover, loosened the scarf around her neck. "It's really
warmer. Warmer! What a difference the sun makes to my
foul nature."

"Oh, not foul at all, I assure you, I feel the same way.
You might want to keep an eye out for a picnic spot,"—
Digby indicated the hotel's carton on the back seat—
"unless you'd prefer a café?"

"Not unless you do. Oh, look—" They passed a herd of
at least a hundred camels, all black, umber; shimmering
silhouettes in the dust-flurried wind as they wound their
way through the sparse, reluctant argan trees that looked
as if they would have preferred to be shrubs, so spare
their spines and leaves, like pen-and-ink drawings.

To their right a long, high roll of land in the distance;
sand dunes down to the invisible sea shown on the road

map on Helen's lap. Vastness of clumped cacti like spiked turbans, an occasional black goat-hair nomad's tent stretched as if a tired bat had settled, leaving wings outspread. Nothing—nothing—nothing—a small white-domed saint's tomb on a scorched hilltop, the eternity of white sky as the kilometers rolled by—nothing—nothing. A green watercourse, full with winter rains now and its banks spread with gaudy laundry, but implicit with summer's shriveling. A truck pulled over on the roadside, the driver on a simple mat kneeling to his prayers. A motorcycle zoomed by, the rider's enormous black turban surmounted by a yellow crash helmet perched on the top like a beanie.

"Stop," Helen said. A palm grove, the trunks half-buried in the sand, flaunted browned and sickened fronds above the wind-pushed dunes that were slowly interring it. "Too good to be ignored?" Digby smiled at her enthusiasm and found a firm enough shoulder for the car, carried their picnic carton behind the blanket Helen was trailing toward a clump of rough trunks.

"You must admit this is the place? Cemeteries are usually good news for picnics, I think. A tree cemetery—okay?"

"Yes." Digby looked hesitant. "If the wind were blowing here I don't know, however. These trees don't look too resilient—falling fronds can be dangerous, you know."

"Oh, piffle, these trees are so buried the fronds aren't high enough to do any damage, and thank heaven there's no wind down here. I can't abide it." Helen spread the blanket and leaned back against a trunk, was sorry. The bark was most unwelcomingly harsh. "Now, let us see. What has the Mamounia given us? Chicken sandwiches, good. Pâté, even better. Olives and tangerines, of course. Aha, deviled eggs, *cornichons!* Very nice indeed. Little cakes and cookies. Wine. Oh, dear, not for me, it makes me so sleepy during the day."

"I too. But just as well, they've forgotten a corkscrew and there are no glasses."

Helen laughed and pulled a plastic bottle of water from her bag, pulled off the seal, and set it between them. "I think, Digby, I'm beginning to get the hang of this country. Be my guest."

She buried the crust of the last sandwich and a tangerine peel in the sand and stretched out in the sun.

Above them the sickly fronds groaned lightly in the air as if, in their sleep, remembering the ancient winds from the west secularly moving the sand toward them and beyond; it was the beyondness that troubled the palms, perhaps. Had they themselves been the wind's ultimate aim this burial alive had a majesty; as it were they were the ignored, of no account, for the wind passed them without malice nor any notice, intent on the mountains far to the east. The palms were mere incidents, collecting their own death from the wind-borne sand about their trunks. Ohhh, ohhh, aah they cried tiredly, but only Helen and Digby were there to hear.

"I say, do forgive me, I didn't know I was so sleepy." Digby sat up and pulled at his hair.

"Don't apologize, you've done all the mountain driving, for one thing, and that took all morning."

"Could I have one of those tangerines? Thanks." He rubbed his face, began peeling the fruit. "We've been in a flap the last few days, about the Center."

"I can imagine. I took some candy and fruit and coffee over for the boys and Kinza and SiOmar yesterday; I'd assumed Abdellatif was an orphan like the rest, but I *think* Kinza was trying to tell me he did have a father somewhere—in the mountains maybe, she kept pointing south. Very confusing, all this Arabic, I can't separate one sound from another. But they're all so sad. SiOmar looks a million years old and she does too. There were a couple of

workmen there, though, putting up safety mesh all
around the pool."

"Oh, yes, Overton got that on the agenda straightaway,
they were very quick about it."

"He's a bit of a sheepdog, isn't he, looking after people?
You said he kept an eye on you all these years, for one
thing, and he has a big reputation as a time-giver as well
as money, from what I've heard. Real fund-raising work,
not just buying tickets to balls, and personnel recruit-
ments and so on."

"Yes indeed. Both within the Enterprises and the other
things. Anyone or anything that pulls its own oar is worth
his attention, it's the layabouts he can't bear. Bores him,
for one thing. He sold off a quite profitable concern a few
years ago because it was doing nothing but raking in
the cash on an old patent, wasn't 'developing and expanding.'"

"I can understand that." A sand beetle ran across Hel-
en's leg, scurried busily away to other business. "He certainly sets a pattern in that area himself. Were he and
your father friends in the army?"

"Oh, no, not at all. He was an aide—very junior, I suppose, but brilliant—to Churchill, Dad was just air trans-
port crewman. Their plane crashed in the sea off Sidi Ifni
—the Spaniards had all that and the Sahara then—three of
them got out, washed up on one of the life rafts, the
Spaniards held them until the end of the war. One of
them died just before, and Dad had been badly shot up;
he did make it home, but not for long, as I told you."

"Was Stanley wounded too?"

"No, not at all. He was on his way to Dakar, some sort
of staff mission, furious at missing the rest of the war. He
said he was more bored than anything. Not, mind you,
that he was idle—he learned very good French and
Spanish from the prisoners and guards. One of them was
Lady—I say, watch it—!"

A moment later Digby pulled himself off Helen's pressed-down body and helped her sit up and brush the sand off her face. A lone frond had given up the ghost and crashed down directly where she'd been sitting.

"Whew—thank you kindly. Damnit, I'd saved the last deviled egg and now it's all sandy. Well, that makes it a definitive picnic, since there weren't any ants. Come on, kid, I'll buy you a coffee in—where's the next town, Tiznit? Goulimine doesn't seem too far on the map, it's only three and we've plenty of time."

"Those!" Helen squealed to herself with glee. The souks in Tiznit were like an enormous clothes closet, with what seemed like all the blue foukiyas in the world hung above the shops and in front. And pillows, pillows in every store, no matter what else, hardware or food or pots and pans. Bolts and bolts of cloth—what a soft place— every version of black, and of white. No visible women, except for one in the distance swathed from head to toe in a vanilla-ice-cream-striped blanket of wool.

"I *must* have a pair," she said aloud to herself, plunging into the store clutching one of the ugliest shoes in the world to her bosom. It had been put with disregard under a pile of prettier slippers outside. Goodyear Tire sole, gray and black coarse suede, vestigial design of a Roman legionary, perhaps, in faded red and yellow leather.

The shopkeeper, who looked none too bright, pushed forward small bins of silver rings and amulets on the counter, ignoring the shoe she was holding out. *"Bonjour, monsieur—ah, non, pas de bagues, merci. Ceci, mais plus long si vous en avez? Non, c'est trop court, vraiment, regardez bien mes pieds.* Damn, I don't think he speaks French. Drat my big American feet, what'll I do?" He was pulling out necklaces, fibulae, bracelets from his shelves.

What, in the gloom of a corner, had looked like a pile of cloth dumped on a low stool said something indistinguishable. The storekeeper turned, answered, smiled with silver teeth, shrugged and went through a thin curtain into a back room. She smiled and nodded at the corner, stood idly trying on rings and finding three that were surprisingly handsome. The merchant, returning with the shoes, smiled at them on her brown, chapped hand. He presented her proudly with two more pairs, but all four for the right foot.

"Oh, God, what now. Character is what these shoes have, back to sign language—" She stopped talking aloud to herself and held up her left foot. The merchant pushed forward a pair of orange embroidered *babouche*.

"No, no." She turned to the dark corner, discerning, now that her eyes were accustomed to the gloom, a dark djellaba with a white snowflake pattern, a little crocheted cap in white. "*Monsieur, pardon, je vous en prie, est-ce que vous parlez Français? Je voudrais bien l'autre, le soulier gauche.*"

"*Il va cherchez, Madame, pas de problem. Ils sont une specialité de Tiznit, les souliers comme ça.*"

"I say, Helen, do you think Lady Overton'd like these, they're quite tiny—" Digby stood in the doorway, the sun on his blond head, holding up a pair of slippers.

"Well, let's see, come on in, the place is full of goodies. What do you think of me in silver, I rather like these rings, and wait'll you see the shoes I've found!" She turned back to the corner to ask the prices, but the curtain to the back of the shop was barely moving. "Well, back to show and tell . . . what d'you feel I should pay for the rings? Damn the Tower of Babel anyway."

Half an hour later they sat in a café, Helen with four rings and her shoes. Digby had had second thoughts—Neva was so very elegant and precise in her tastes. He ruffled through a dozen postcards he'd bought, ordered coffee.

"Sell me a couple, will you, I feel like being sociable."

She tapped her pen against her teeth, picked out a view of a camel munching cactus and scribbled on it to Arthur:

And you think *you* have trouble with your diet. Am being as relentless as the I.R.S. More later.

Mata

"Oh, look at that girl getting into the Club Med car from Agadir over there—I saw her back in the souks and thought it was Debbysue Kemp with that wonderful hair. Pretty. She seemed a very ⟨thoroughly⟩ nice girl. Well, what do I owe you? One to Marrakech and one air to England—four dirhams? Outrageous. *En route, en route,* dusk approaches."

Digby was busy with stamps. She passed him her second card, a somewhat depressing view of a mud house with many scrawny goats in the foreground. Scrawled on the back was:

Dere Simon, Wen are you cuming bak to I and the childrun?

Velveeta Mae

CHAPTER VI

It was always difficult for new arrivals, when they had brushed past the plastic *portiere rideau* into the bar of the Hotel Elfrieda and survived Fräulein's acid-eyed inspection, to determine whether the ancient trumpet vine in the garden court beyond the dining room was holding up the hotel, or vice-versa. The vine itself was so very unlikely in the arid, dehydrated little town; it had been trained on long-disappeared trellises to avoid the overhead sunblasts of summer and had somehow prospered over the decades. A marriage with a sturdy bougainvillea gave it shade as well, and some moisture was kept around the stunted banana trees, hibiscus, dwarf palmettos and oleanders beneath.

Had the hotel been run by a Moroccan it would have been quite predictably squalid as well as uncomfortable. As it was, Fräulein had—if not vision—remembrance of other places, perhaps, other standards. Each room of the twenty she reigned over was provided with a towel, for one thing, even the simple rooms upstairs with only a washbasin. The sole toilet reigned above all, reached by a separate stair discreetly leading to the chamber on the roof wherein it sat on a dais, wooden seated and usually quite clean, with a water tank and chain and, in case of drought, a very large and heavy zinc watering can to provide the necessary *chasse d'eau*. Paper was provided.

Her best rooms were downstairs at the foot of the garden court and the side; they all opened only onto the garden and four of them were furnished in the very best style of a bridal suite on a Turkish freighter, with small sitting alcoves overstuffed with banquettes and a plastic coffee table, and the very best available plush hangings depicting the eruption of Etna, Notre Dame at night, prowling lions with palms, views of Mecca from the air, pairs of peacocks, and the Taj Mahal. Bedside lamps existed, shaded in torn silk; two coat hangers were provided; and numbers 18 and 19 had not only basins and bidets but, respectively, shower and tub.

Occupants of the downstairs rooms soon learned that naps in the late afternoon were not comfortable. Fraülein did a ringing illegal trade in alcohol for the men of the town who came in to smoke their kif pipes and drink beer and whiskey. The chief of police was fond of Stork, Tuborg, Flag indiscriminately. Everyone was well behaved and reasonably discreet; there was no trouble. However, conversation in the little garden increased in vigor as the evening approached, and unless one was willing to stifle in airlessness with closed windows—the rooms became unbearably dank immediately, even in high summer—the fumes of kif and the loosened tongues discouraged sleep until Fräulein stood in the archway to the garden and banged on a brass tray. By eight the garden was empty.

Fräulein Elfrieda had some mystery, and some history, and not much was known about either. Whence, for instance, came the quite definite corset, with strings, laces, bones, straps, that revealed its sturdy outline under her dresses? She never left the town, and such garments, even as stoutly made as hers, do not last forever in a place where one perspires a great deal of the year. Sent away for, no doubt, with yearly increasing measurements, from as far as Marseilles. Fräulein was not the sort to frivol away her money in Zurich, to be sure.

Fräulein's table in the dining room, which opened onto the bar as well as the garden at the other end, was war room, desk, gaming board, and the surface on which her never-ending knitting was blocked, as well as her perch for the television, which received snowflake patterns very clearly. Nevertheless, the set was turned on for dinner—served strictly and only from seven-thirty to nine and not a crumb before nor after. Occasionally the face of the King broke through, or a torch singer in cut-on-the-bias satin. Once an ice-skating exposition from France had materialized for a riveting twelve minutes. December in the dining room proclaimed itself by dessicated ribbons strung from the ceiling, and Joyeux Noël written carefully in soap on the mirror over the buffet.

There were no exceptions to anything, and supplements to pay for everything. Water was often turned off throughout Goulimine for conservation; Fräulein had her own arrangement with the *chef de service* (he liked scotch) and was in possession of her own wrench and key, allowing her to have water when she felt it was appropriate. None of those times had anything to do with the cleanliness or convenience of her guests. But the garden flourished.

She was discreet during Ramadan, and only served the pasha, the chief of police, and the governor of the province. Since she had the only liquor anywhere for many, many kilometers, the rest of her clients observed the holy month willy-nilly.

The town was accustomed to her, and she no longer needed the strictly tourist clientele that had once come in the days of the French Protectorate to the great camel souks, or the travelers stopping for their last European meal before entering the now-closed Sahara. She had refused to make an arrangement with any of the day-trip buses that came down from Agadir, thus forcing them to return to Tiznit for lunch. She rarely left the hotel, and what indeed was there for her to leave for—there was no cinema, no one she need talk to. She gleaned from the kif smokers what news she needed. Her thin, pearly-white skin with its damp sheen bloomed in the dimness of the bar with its coffee machine, the oasis of her garden court, and Helen privately thought, as she stepped out into the square, that if she could have devised a bead curtain at the entrance that resembled a spider's web she would have done so.

"No, I only take pictures of my friends wearing funny hats, for pleasure."

"You don't have a camera with you, when you travel?" Fergus asked.

"Nope. It takes all the fun out of it for me. I'm always seeing potential photographs and never the object itself, or the person. Like this." She waved her hand at the square in front of the Café Charazade. "Heaven not to have to do a damn thing with it, to it, for it, about it. Just enjoy and look. What marvelously brigandish looks they have, don't they? Moustaches like pistols. How was your trip yesterday? As nice as Digby's and mine, I hope."

"Handsome, handsome." Fergus was speaking of Helen as well as his drive with Erica and his crew of two assistants in the pair of small vans down from Taroudannt. Helen had picked up some swarthy color in the last few days, waiting for them to disentangle themselves from price disputes with the unused and disgruntled camel men in Taroudannt, Stanley prying Neva from the swimmable pool and playable tennis courts in the sunny warmth of the Gazelle d'Or. "It's all quite handsome, I must come back on holiday, like you, and see it with my own eye."

"Do. Lucky me. I've been rattling around wherever I could on all the little tracks and *pistes* and lanes; there's a charming little rascal, Sherif, who'd like to go with me more often than I let him, but he's useful in urging me on to delights I wouldn't find otherwise. You must come with me. I may have found a location for you."

"Don't get your hopes up, there's no point in looking for a thing for this ridiculous bit until his lordship arrives, anything we find won't be the ticket, I guarantee you."

"Well, you didn't miss anything yesterday morning—camel souk on Saturdays, you know? Dig and I went and there were a handful of camels, one bogus blue man, and three enormous tour buses down from Agadir. Up at the crack of dawn, they must have been—out of the bus, take their pictures, shiver shiver, it was cold, back to the bus, come into town for a look at the junk jewelry and a quick Fanta, back in the bus—"

"Yes, we saw them having horrible greasy tajines in Tiznit on our way down—back to Agadir for dinner. That's a long long way just to see some sad camels. Four hundred kilometers."

"Anyway, I hope Stanley's not going to be too fussy—an awful lot of things around here are bright green just now, and while the rains have stopped for a time little Sherif tells me they'll be back, abundantly. Hard to think it's December, though, today."

"Same around Tiznit—perfect ramparts but not one speck of them clear of telephone or electric wires and all. Even if I could mask those with palm fronds you can't paint the fields brown. And of course *that's* no good." Fergus glared at the ruins of a fortress on the hilltop; the little town had crawled up toward it and the remains of the fort had crumbled into unphotogenic decay in any event. "And he says he has to have ramparts. Ah, here's the crew."

Fergus's assistants, Philip and Maurice, had driven up with Erica between them and parked in front of the hotel.

"Lunch here, I think, it'll be too late for the hotel." Erica had tied up her hair in a dull scarf, and her long sleeves and wide pajama-cut trousers were dusty, her face and hands unornamented. "Let me just go into the kitchen and see what's on." The young men dropped into empty chairs, took one from the next table for Erica. She came back, ticking off the menu on a finger.

"Beef or camel tajine, vegetable couscous, salad—which will be cold potatoes, beets, carrots, half a hard-boiled egg."

"Camel for me, please." Helen grinned at Fergus, who winced. "Well, I want to try it." Everyone else opted for couscous; Erica asked for salad alone and a bottle of water.

"So," Fergus asked, wiping the bottom of his plate with a piece of bread, "have you found camels? Riders? Gofers and grips? If not, why not?"

"Wonder Woman here has," Philip said. "With Kauder it seemed as if one could only get two things done a day, and if the first thing wasn't accomplished somehow the second couldn't be, even if they were totally unrelated. Erica, however, has disabused me of that idea." She smiled, lit a cigarette, and called the young waiter over for coffee, tea—did anyone want an orange, yogurt?

"Don't be all that hopeful, Philip. Everyone is excited about 'les films' and 'le publicite,' but it'll be when Stanley produces Jouti's letters to the pasha that things'll really get going. I wonder if the army keeps any camels down here—it would have been a snap in Zagora, they have herds of them there. Well, if they do and we can use them, it'll be a walk. The going price, today at least, is a hundred dirhams a day for rider with camel, with food. A bit more if they do their own cooking. Horses the same."

"Don't bristle, Ferg," Maurice put in. "I didn't think we wanted horses either, but it seems any mid-length to long shot of a herd of camels galloping across the desert in style has to have outriding horses outside the frame. Camels seem to have a mind of their own; the old boy Erica found assures us he worked on Lawrence of Arabia and knows what he's talking about."

"Ah, well. At least the famous blue isn't in short supply. I had my doubts when we got in yesterday." It had been cold, windy, gritty; the little town had looked unutterably dreary to Fergus, all the men in poor, sad, brown and gray, shabby wool djellabas. Now, in the warmth and the sun, the square sparkled with blue, draas hanging in folds from shoulders and tied at the ankle-length hems in knots, more blue foukiyas beneath, great massive desert turbans of blue or black.

"Yes, well,"—Erica sipped at her coffee, sent it back for more milk curtly—"you'll still be glad I brought the cloth I did. My indigo is the real thing and I was right, you can't get it here anymore. And any you find being worn will be unutterably filthy."

"Where's Overton, Ferg?" Maurice peeled slowly and carefully at a small, thick orange. "Everyone talks about the rain coming back, it's too bad to hang about like this. Wasn't he supposed to come along with us yesterday?"

"Of course." Fergus looked across the square at a pair of women, draped from head to toe in black haiks with a tiny white star pattern, their silhouettes oddly like Tanagra figurines, high-crowned and graceful, the ends of the haiks on their shoulders tied to rings of heavy housekeys to keep the wind from disturbing the covering of their faces. "But I am not privy to his lordship's whereabouts. He will arrive in due course and we might as well enjoy our leisure. Perhaps I shall go back to the hotel and get roundly drunk this afternoon with all the locals."

"Oh, don't, it's much too nice a day, save that for the rain." Helen burped suddenly.

"Is that the camel that speaks? How was it?"

"Divine. Sheer grease and stringy meat and carrots like cotton wool. Exactly, exactly like my aunt's pot roast. Erica, what is going on with your coffee? That's the third time you've sent it back."

"Such a nuisance, but I do like it the way I want it and

Mohammed DumbDumb here refuses to get the idea. *A ulidi! Nouss-nouss!*" She was almost hissing as the little boy in a dirty apron picked up the dark glass with burnt umber-colored coffee now replaced with what looked like pure milk. "Half and half! *Nouss-nouss! NOUSS-NOUSS!*" The boy sighed, took it away. "Well, Fergus, if you're at a loose end that's all right, but I must hit the souks in search of cloth for other projects as well as yours —no point being down here and not seeing what's been smuggled in lately, is there? Helen, you're coming? Anything any of you need, anyone want to join us?"

"No, I think the boys and I had better get over to the hotel and work on that second camera that's sticking, there's plenty to do in terms of what we've shot already. Maurice, you'd better see to getting that punctured spare tire mended as well."

"No, no tomobil today, Sherif, maybe tomorrow." Helen had bought a small tin of Nivea cream from a barrow and was rubbing it into her hands; they had red welts on them as if some insect had bitten her. She and Sherif had trailed behind Erica into what seemed like a hundred cloth shops, all of which had every possible color of blue and white cotton. And sheets: as in Tiznit with pillows, everyone here seemed to specialize in sheets, ladies using them as haiks, Yves St. Laurent stripes mingling over the vegetable barrows with Wamsutta spring floral prints. All with their curious high-crowned silhouettes and bunches of keys, it was charming, charming.

The little boy in his huge blue turban and ragged djellaba looked downcast at the news there would be no drive in the country today, but after all, there were the film people now, not just this strange lady, and the *camionnettes;* he would be in the film, a movie star, she was their friend and would arrange it all. He would have a passport and go to France and have a bicycle.

Helen found Erica sitting on a straw-matted floor in a shallow shop front, fingering *coupons* of cloth and talking with a young Berber merchant with a serene, almost oriental, face. She sat down on the high sill, swinging one leg, watching young Sherif cross the street at the merchant's instructions to bring back the inevitable tray of tea. A nice kid, bright, he's picked up some English, some German. What'll happen to him? He's young enough to yearn, and not quite old enough to settle. About twelve, very likely.

Erica was deep in negotiations as far as Helen could tell from body language; Arabic still sounded like a bad case of postnasal drip, utterly foreign, although she was beginning to pick out a few sounds, a word or two from Sherif. Helen felt diffident about interrupting Erica to ask about the two draas that were hanging from the wall —Simon might like one, and she herself, perhaps.

Strange, she thought dreamily, her head full of cloth dust and sleepy from too much lunch, she was spending a lot of time on clothes, and that wasn't her style. Aside from comfort and being presentable enough to get accomplished what she set out to do, she'd settled for what she thought of as a "uniform" long ago, repeating the same sweaters, skirts, pants. Well, she had little to do at the moment, floating. It was all strange, and clothes were universal reassurance, they touched one's body, became one's first environment from nightgowns to ballgowns; they stood between you and the world in any language. Besides, it was fun.

She quietly got up, stretched, took down one of the draas from its hanger. A small turtle was moving slowly across the matting, pulling its head into its shell in the sun. The merchant smiled, picked it up, set it carefully under his sewing machine. Helen slipped the draa over her head. It was simply a large square folded over with a head hole that plunged in a truncated V neckline to a square pocket on the chest. She gathered the yards of cloth that were hanging well below her hands and arranged them in folds on her shoulders, as she had seen the men wear them in the square. The open sides were stitched for five inches at the hem on the floor; great for sleeping, for over a bathing suit, for making love and all sorts of things.

"He says it looks well on you—it does, I wouldn't have thought that blue would. Are you interested? I'll see what it's going for."

"Two, please, I've a friend—this other, the old one, it's beautiful."

"Yes, it'll set you back considerably more. I'll see what I can do."

Helen admired herself in a sliver of mirror, showed off to a giggling Sherif on the doorsill, while Erica resumed her conversation, indicating several lengths of cloth she had set to one side. *"Arba alaf,"* Erica kept repeating politely but firmly, *"arba alaf,"* with a charming smile; the man nodded finally, hands outspread, smiled back. Apparently they were discussing the two draas now, the old one in Erica's lap as she pointed out defects, a small stain. As Helen pulled her head from the second robe, he said with some resignation, *"Wakha, lalla, tnash er mia, u arba alaf."*

"Well, that's not so bad, Helen, five thousand rials— that's two hundred and fifty dirhams for the old one, it's a beauty, and sixteen hundred rials, that's eighty dirhams for the other, really quite good. You'd better take it. There aren't any further north, so it's now or never. He thinks they're part of my order, you see, which is why the price is good. No, no, pay *me* at the hotel, will you, he'll only get confused."

Erica stepped down from the sill, the draas and her cloth wrapped and tied into a large parcel, and beckoned to Sherif, who was standing on one foot looking at her quietly. "Have this little brat of yours carry them, Helen, he's got nothing better to do." But Sherif looked sadly at Helen for a moment, turned, and ran.

Helen stood in the cement shower stall under the stairs that ordinary guests were meant to share, and felt for the third time the water grudgingly issuing from the tap. Lukewarm, still. She had asked if she could have hot water at six, before she'd gone out for lunch. The waiter had assured her there would be no problem, but there would, alas, be a supplement of five dirhams. Of course, she'd assured him, but hot water at six.

Now she heard Fräulein outside nattering at one of the maids. Putting her head outside the door, she clutched her robe around her and called.

Fräulein waddled over to the door, her dyed black hair showing purple in the twilight, the old scalp gleaming through the tonsure point. "Yes, you called? What is the trouble?"

"Fräulein, the hot water for which I asked at midday to be ready now—there is none."

"Impossible." Elfrieda brushed through the door into the shower stall, put her hand under the drizzle coming from the tap. "*Voila*. That is the hot water *robinet*. Therefore, that is hot water. *Safi!*"

"I do hope the bossman's picking up the tab for our drink—*never* have I paid so much and gotten so little, although after a cold shower it's worth it." Helen swirled the dollop of whiskey left in the bottom of her glass and sighed.

"Bossman or not, have another. I smell dinner becoming imminent." Fergus nodded to the waiter for a fresh drink for them and pulled a stool out for Philip, who had come in through the door from the square.

"Ho there, folks. I say, Helen, your little sidekick's outside, I think he wants to see you, but he won't come in."

Sherif was indeed outside, drawing arabesques with a finger in the dust on one of the vans.

"Hi, Sherif, come on in and have a Coca or a Fanta?"

"Fräulein no like, angry *bzeff*. We go tomobil tomorrow?"

"*Inch'allah*. We wait for big boss to come from Taroudannt."

"Good he come tomorrow. Rain some days soon." He was worried about something, she could see. The stars were beginning to come out, as big as soup plates in the darkening sky.

"That lady Rhikya from Marrakech, she no your friend?" He looked warily up at Helen, puffing on a surreptitious cigarette butt.

"Erica? Why—I hope so, Sherif. I don't know her well, but she's helped me a lot. Why do you ask?"

"My uncle—SiBrahim in hanout today—he say her draas you buy *tnash er miat* rials—there twenny rials one dirham so that *steen* dirhams, sixish—no, *sixty*. And old one, *arba alaf* rials, that *miatayn* dirhams, *two honnerd*. But she tell you they *tmaneen* dirhams, that eightish, no, *eighty*, and *miatayn u khamseen*, that *two honnerd feefty*. I think she *no* your friend. We go tomobil tomorrow, I teach you money in Arabiya, you learn quick, *wakha?*"

"I see." She found a five-dirham note in her pocket, a whole dollar and more. "Take this, honey, for tonight's lesson, and we go tomobil tomorrow. *Baraka llaufik*, Sherif, I have one friend, anyway."

Neva Overton ran the gamut of the hot-eyed men beginning to fill the garden court, and found Stanley ahead of her directing her baggage into the farthest corner, number 18. He was next door in 19, closer to the tables and the beer drinkers. Oh, dear, she thought, if we could only have stayed on at the Gazelle in Taroudannt. The two couches that almost filled the minuscule sitting alcove were rigidly hard, the bed beyond the arch was ominously spoon-shaped and mushy looking. Well, never mind. "Darling, how cute—I'll need several more clothes hangers, and no doubt you will too."

"Right away, old girl. Colorful, isn't it? Don't know about the plumbing, but we'll manage, I daresay."

"Of course. Oh, it seems one must book ahead for a bath. Fräulein's getting some hot water organized, but what a tartar! Made jolly sure I knew there was a supplement—am I being extravagant?"

Stanley laughed, tipped the porter. "Violently, my love, but I shan't object if you'll let me scrub your back. Want the tub in my rooms?"

"Not today, this little shower is fine. Is everyone here, d'you know? I assume this *is* the only hotel?"

"It's the hotel, such as it is, and everyone's here. Digby's in number twelve, he left a message for me he was off with Erica doing Polaroid tests for photogenic faces and so forth. Come along then, just time for a late lunch, I must take that letter from Jouti over to the pasha, we want to get started as soon as we can. There's not much for you to do here, for one thing."

"Oh, I'll be fine, darling. I've my needlepoint as usual, and Digby and I have all the Christmas cards to do, you know I'm never at a loose end with you."

"God bless." He pulled a chair out from a table in the dining room for her, settled himself. "Ah, garçon, yes. Two omelets, salad, bottle of white wine, please."

"Stanley, I'm so glad you took time to show me Tafraoute and all those other places. The light and those rocks there, fairyland. What was the name of the beach with the lagoon and flamingos?"

"Massa. Yes, Massa's definitely on. It'll take some arranging to get around that nature preserve or whatever, but that's Jouti's end of it. Bad water problem at Tafraoute, you saw that hotel's pool, empty and cracked, clearly never used. To my mind we might do better to have a super job on the beach outside Tiznit, and a restaurant up in Tafraoute for day trips."

"Oh, for heaven's sake, truck water up for a pool if you must, there's no place like it. I do agree Tiznit could use a proper hotel, it's such a scary place, all soldiers and walls, harsh. But that's only me, I know. It's going to be very exciting. I do wish Arthur had been well enough to come down with us, I should think he'd be bursting with ideas by now."

"Yes, well, between you and me, darling, there may be a hitch or two there. Jouti may very well have something up his sleeve, a friend of his own, we'll have to see. Now, back to my muttons . . . no, no, you stay and have a coffee. I want to find the pasha between naps. Here are some dirhams to go on with—shall we meet back here at six, six-thirty? The souks are just across the square, I think; see what you can find that'll be nice for the new villa, hmm?"

"Of course. But—Stanley, there aren't any locks on the windows in our rooms, d'you think at night—I must have *some* air?"

"Darling, darling little Neva, all will be well. I should think those chaps in the garden would be so grateful for their forbidden drink, the last thing they'd do is rock the boat, and one look at Fräulein Elfrieda should reassure you, if nothing else. That sad little guerrilla war is hundreds of kilometers away, and you know I'd never take you anyplace dangerous anyway. Now, silver jewelry's the thing to look for down here, I'm told—"

She smiled ruefully, the fine travel-dusted skin around her lovely deep-set eyes crinkling, and patted his jacket with a gold-ringed hand. "Of course, you've coddled me for so long I'm spoiled. And the countryside has been so . . . desolate, somehow, on the way down, it quite dampened my spirits until now. But we're going to have fun, I know."

She stepped out into the rocky glare of the square, which was coming alive in the early afternoon light. An ominous number of army troop carriers full of soldiers were starting up and pulling out of their parking area, grim khaki and camouflage paint, sad cheap uniforms on the boys, sand goggles around their necks. Oh, dear, so very young, so very young. Odd Stanley didn't seem interested in any sort of excursion over to Sidi Ifni to see where he'd been a prisoner during the war; from the map and her Michelin it seemed it had a stupendous beach and that alone should interest him for the hotels. He was such a forward looker, perhaps he'd put down unpleasant memories, take her over if there were a rainy day. How curious it was, if it hadn't been for the Spanish prison camp she'd never have met him at all, she would very likely be selling frocks to middle-aged ladies in some dreary shop; certainly she would never have arrived on the edge of a desert by herself.

The gendarme dropped his arm as the last of the transports pulled away. The square resumed its blue bustling, the men hawk-faced, moustachioed, glitter-eyed. Were they taller than the men in Marrakech, or was it only the great mass of their turbans that made her feel even smaller than usual? Certainly duller, in her beige suede safari jacket and trousers with a white pullover beneath. She was the color of the dry little town itself, with its splashes of whitewash on the ocher houses. No, this is not my place, I don't belong here—all washed-dust colors, gold with the joy gone out of it, like me, like me, she thought with rising panic. A cocoon, I need a cocoon and it disappears when Stanley isn't with me.

She forced herself to cross the street, past a sidewalk café with men drinking tea. Café Charazade—I could not last a thousand and one hours in a place like this, not to say nights. Thank God for the little garden in the hotel, it almost reminds me of Barbados, my own hibiscus, bougainvillea. She did not know if she were pleased or irritated that, aside from the dark slit eyes of the tea drinkers, she was being ignored. There were no boys, young men, plucking at her arm as they did so maddeningly every minute one was out in Marrakech, murmuring in their nasal monotones "I yam not a guide I yam a stoodent" and never *ever* leaving one alone, forcing one back with unspent money and unbought delights because of their importunity.

She turned right, hesitantly, a miniature arcade on one side with seated ladies, their backs against a wall and in front of their many spread-out black skirts were cloths laden with jewelry, beads, headdresses, amulets, dubious-looking coral, amber, ivory, shells, a thousand hands of Fatima in distressing filigree, red glass chunks wired into the palms. Men were squatting in front, pushing ornaments around contemptuously, the butter-soft brown hands of the ladies palm outward, expostulating, pulling rings of worth off their own fingers as prizes not available to just anyone, Sidi, you understand that—

Barrows of resinous incense puffed little clouds into the dry air, young boys looked longingly at bins of pocket-knives, tiny boxes of Tide, mirrors, bottles of rose water, plastic combs, picture frames, jumbles of cassettes.

A trio of stocky, madras-plaid tourists were blocking the arcade, having persuaded an enormous man in a ferocious black turban that covered his neck, chin, and nose as well as his head, and with a curved silver dagger hanging from his blue robes, to pose for three of the several cameras they had around their necks. A woman with a dark haik leaving visible only her eyes, which were cast modestly down, and a hand heavy with silver rings, stood behind him to one side. Unlike her, the ladies of the little souk were not veiled; how dark and sparkling they are, Neva thought, and how nice to see their faces— Marrakech was full of walking ghosts, in contrast.

The cameras clicked and crackled in enthusiasm; one of the photographers attempted to have the lady stand next to the man, but she refused, shaking her dark wrapped head and keeping humbly in the background. "Thank you, *shokrane*, thank you thank you." Coins were pressed into the large man's hand, he looked at them, shook his head, held up five fingers. Shrugging, the tourists rummaged through their change, added more, and screwing on their lens caps, sauntered off to a waiting car elatedly. "Yes, that's the real thing, all right, should print up beautifully."

"Neva Overton! You're here!" The black turban was being unswathed, yard by yard, and gathered up by a laughing little boy in a shabby djellaba as Fergus's face appeared. The souk ladies began their high-pitched ululation like a chorus of insane birdsong, clapping their hands in rhythmic delight and helping Helen remove the black floss-wound armature that had held her haik off the top of her head and given her the graceful, nodding silhouette of the town.

"Neva," Helen gasped, shaking herself free of the folds of cloth, "let me tell you, hot isn't the word for it under one of those—this is no country to be a woman in. Did you just get here? How elegant you do look. Come on into this little hanout, we've been horsing around with SiHassan and the ladies, they seem to think if we try on their wares we're bound to buy them. But we did fool the tourists, poor things. How much did you make them give you, Fergus? Five dirhams? Super. No, Lalla, I don't know what I'd do with it if I bought it." She smiled, handing the armature back to an enormous dark lady who smiled back, put it among her collection of cowrie shells and blue glass beads.

Neva followed them into the narrow, dusky shop, where trays of tea, glasses filmed with yogurt stood about among the merchant's cluttered collection. "We've been hanging out here for hours," Fergus said happily, "starving this poor man out, he's clearly weakening at the thought of getting rid of us and home to a proper meal. Too polite to eject us, though. So look about and let's strike while hunger gnaws at his vitals. Helen's after two camel bags and a string of silver beads. I bags the brass tray and the Koran box, and possibly this dagger that got us into those clothes to begin with."

SiHassan smiled weakly, pulled out a low stool for Neva while Helen and Fergus plunked themselves down on the floor, pawing through their choices in front of them. He unstrung long looped leather thongs, hundreds of rings fell from them onto the little rug he had placed at her feet. Oh, dear, she knew nothing of them, what to look for, what made them of worth, but one must learn, she was expected to take an interest. They fell from her slender fingers back onto the floor, mixing themselves hopelessly, she lost sight of one that had seemed pretty.

"No, no, thank you, but I don't wear silver, you see." Still, the bracelet he had put on her wrist was like nothing she had seen, heavy with knobs and bumps, perhaps she could have it gold plated? It was a bone she could lay at Stanley's feet, witness that she had coped, taken part. He was showing her old ceramic bowls, they must have been lovely once, but all chipped. Stanley would never stand a crack or imperfection. SiHassan's stomach gave a loud growl as he put more rings on her fingers, a string of amber around her neck.

"Perhaps then this bracelet?"—she turned to Helen helplessly—"and a brass stirrup? It would make into a lamp, you see?"

"Very nicely, too. Okay, kids, we're down to the wire, this poor man is going to faint dead away in a minute.

Sherif, *sahabti,* my friend, where are we with the rials and dirhams now?"

"Ah, he say for *culshi,* everything, with new lady things, *alaf* dirhams."

"A *thousand dirhams?* Insane. He's out to lunch."

Sherif turned to SiHassan and translated rapidly.

"He say he *not* out to lunch, but he say he wish he were."

CHAPTER VII

Helen turned off the ignition and climbed out of her little car, swallowed up in the silence. She stood squinting into the early morning sun, at the cracked clay earth that crinkled its way to the distance, toward the feather-duster palms that marked *"le source"* little Sherif had been so sure they would want for *"le film."* The flatness, the scentless and dustless air, the stillness—she knew if she turned around she could see the dun and umber foothills of the Anti Atlas, a measurable location of where she was. They would be on a map, many maps, but this stretch before her, no map would want it, need it.

Stanley's glittering car and the two vans were pulled up close to the wall of Ait Bouchka, curious shy children watching the film makers, led by Erica and Khalifa Rachid. The khalifa had been instantly assigned by the pasha to assist Lord Overton in any possible way, and had eagerly complied. He was a young man from Fès, which Helen gathered was the Boston of Morocco, since he had little but contempt for life on the edge of the desert.

She leaned against the fender of her car, the warm engine making clicking noises. Sherif had shown her, a few days ago, the little fort on a hill of sand, they had seen the low mud houses and slanting doorjambs that looked like truants from Egypt, the shy women fluttering their black skirts around corners, supple bronze hands slamming shut crude tamarisk-wood doors, the stretch of wall to the east with eroding merlons and crenels guarding against— against, that was enough to know.

Stanley had stopped short of the gate, was holding forth to Fergus and pointing. She couldn't hear their words, but Philip was nodding, Maurice writing something on a clipboard. Erica had set down the bag of sugar cones she had brought as a gift to the shaykh and was looking at the walls. Stanley stopped, turned, and strode back to his car, made a large swing on the cracked soil and passed Helen at a distance, in the direction of Goulimine.

He must have liked it, she thought, or they'd all be coming back as well. The crew turned back toward the village and went up the small sandy hill to the opening in the wall, so basic it could only be called a gate with imagination. The dust from Stanley's car became a thin, pale plume over her shoulder. Dear heaven, where was the man off to now? He'd apparently done some sort of a marathon with Neva on their trip down from Taroudannt, she'd gone over her road map idly this morning, waiting for the others to finish breakfast. Little dots on dirt tracks, Tizourhine, Tiffermit, Assaka, Oued Massa, Tagannt—others she couldn't remember. No wonder Neva was spending the morning recuperating. Perhaps Stanley was trying to replace divots with her today, although how he'd amuse her—the hotel was the only place that would have anything faintly resembling an amusing little luncheon, for instance.

How nice it would be for Fergus if this were finally the place; no green at all on this side, very desert-looking, although the ramparts weren't exactly in the Beau Geste league. But the oasis Sherif was so proud of was right out of a Maria Montez-Jon Hall movie, if clichés were wanted.

Helen, who with Sherif had been given tea in the shaykh's mud-floored dark house, felt she could do without indoors this morning, the squatting on little stools, the shaven-headed courteous shaykh lengthily rinsing the tea-

pot, breaking a sugar cone with a brass hammer, the
steeping, tossing dregs on the floor, the endless sipping,
sipping, and always the knowledge that ripe olive eyes
dark with kohl were peering through cracks in doors behind one.

Much too nice out here; the sheer quiet was enough.
Fräulein Elfrieda did close up the hotel tightly at ten-
thirty, but could do nothing about a pack of wild dogs
somewhere in the distance, and surely would do nothing
about her terrible beds. Whoever was in number 8 next to
Helen had sounded ill all night long as well, dark groans
and coughs; the wind had come up around midnight, and
with a Venturi effect troubled the palmettos and vines,
their leaves scratching in botanical quarrels.

She pulled at the blanket in the trunk, which was
partly rumpled under her bags from London she hadn't
taken into the hotel, she knew the contents must be still
damp and muddy from Crumbles; she should give them
to one of the maids and have them washed. The bags
crumpled forward as she yanked at the blanket, and behind them a sleek leather case toppled over, spilling
papers out as she pulled.

She settled herself on the blanket in the sun and gathered all the papers together, remembering she'd been in
an ugly hassle with the parking *guardien* at the airport
when the porter had put her long-lost duffels into the
trunk for her. He must have seen the London-Marrakech
tag on this case and assumed it was hers as well. Digby,
how glad he'd be, it was the missing file case he was an-
guishing so much over. With good reason, she thought—
Stanley wouldn't be compassionate about contretemps
such as this one. She riffled her hand over the neatly la-
beled upright files, the smell of expensive pigskin exotic
around her. Well, let's see where these go. Press releases
with color reproductions of the painting Stanley was
going to give to the Center—an unfinished oil sketch, ac-

tually, but there the Center's buildings were in the foreground, blue grilles on the kitchen door and Debbysue's window upstairs. A pity in a way it was going to hang there—so few people would see it. Still, it might draw a few rich Moroccans who otherwise wouldn't go near the place, and jog them into giving a donation or two. Shaking the dust off the brochures, she thought it generous of Stanley; he must have been a very young man during his brief time with Churchill, and remember it vividly. It would have been natural of him to keep the thing, particularly with the added cachet of Churchill's giving it to him himself.

King's Road. What a long way away all that seemed. Stanley seemed to own some real estate there; the folder had spilled out leases for shops, rental schedules. You'd think he'd have all that taken care of by a screamingly junior minion or two—it looked like very small potatoes except for the location. Braid Trade—wasn't that the boutique Erica had said she'd been having such trouble with? Helen had a faint memory of it herself, ankling around Chelsea trying to find a typewriter repairman who would make a house call to Simon's little flat on Church Street.

Bettman, Marrakech. Wow! Helen had no compunction about seizing what the gods offered, and never had. Oh, dear, all this was about the villa though, estimates in French from a local builder, she didn't want to try to noodle out those and saw there was no need, they'd all been sent to Stanley by Arthur in the spring anyway. Receipts for land taxes, a note in Arthur's heavy script from Marbella, saying he'd be in Marrakech if the Overtons were coming down as usual. Well, wait, a handwritten list of place names, some crossed out definitely, some with a question mark, one—Tata—with "the worst place in the world" scrawled beside it. Most of them began and ended in t . . . Tiznit, Tagannt, Tagmoute, Tan-Tan—that had had a famous beach during the great hippie days, and beaches were in increasingly short supply. Ah, Todra Gorge, and a note beside it referring to A.B. Splendid. But so many little places that were just dots on the road? Well, perhaps there was water, and one could create an oasis of all delights, who knew about resort hotels anymore.

A bill of some sort, for an oil portrait, £500; attached was a color print of a painting of a middle-aged man in a gray suit, clerical collar, hair beginning to fade, a hint of a cloister in the background. A note on the foot of the bill about wanting the other six if they were available—six of what, she wondered?—and what should be done with this, he would hold it for instructions. And acknowledging payment of £1500 for oil landscape per description. She put it back in the Bettman-Marrakech file, thought that Digby'd better get his act together, anything less Arthurish or Moroccan there wasn't.

Still, not much about the hotels, not even a file to itself. One for "Barbados," some Overton Enterprises writing paper, an address book, files for "Aunt Sarah," "Zippy," "Leather Export." She closed the case and lay back in the still morning air. Not really surprising, though, there were stages in any of these deals—particularly in a country like this—where the less there was in writing, the better. How enormous the sky was.

"Talk about Cecil B. De Mille! You mean he's really having more ramparts built as well as repairing the old ones? Isn't this a little bit on the loony side, Ferg? No, pour out—my luggage always goes 'slosh-slosh' when I travel in Islam."

Fergus darkened his drink and lay back on Helen's bed, glowering at the opposite wall. "He is indeed having merlons and crenels added, and something whorish done to the gate in case we want to have a charge of camels issuing forth from the fort. Well, that only involves buckets of mud, essentially, but on top of that he wants a second go with tents—not, mind you, the goat-hair tents around here, but very expensive party tents trucked down from Agadir—the ones with the black and white designs, you know, brass knobs on top. Why oh why do company directors not go skiing, I ask you. Or prospecting for oil on their holidays? Perhaps you could arrange for him to be kidnapped by the Algerians? I'd really think he was a bit soft in the head if he weren't so damned nice, so fair. He made a heavy point with the khalifa that the shaykh was to get whatever was appropriate for our using the village, but on top of that—since he knows damn well most of it'll stay right in the shaykh's pocket—the head of each family is to be rounded up and given something as well. Decent. The whole village is delirious, sure they're all going to be rich and famous and get enough to go to Mecca."

"That is nice of him, the family bit. Listen, you have to be sure to give my Sherif a job, okay? I did anticipate your need for booze, so I felt free to promise him. Oh, booze—Digby's been assigned to borrow my little car and take Neva up to Agadir for the night tomorrow morning, he's accepting orders for things from *pharmacies* and *epiceries* and so on, such as scotch and brandy. Wish he could bring *me* down a hot bath, that's what she's going for, that and her hair, you must let me know if I begin to pong."

"Can't tell over my own ripe odors. What's next door, anyway? An unoiled hinge?"

"Somebody sick, I think. I don't know. Little trays of tea and water go to and fro. Oh, speaking of invalids, Arthur called just before you got back and he sounds almost possible. Essayed an omelet at one of the countesses' and no dire consequences. Managed a morning in the rug souk without dying of fatigue, and got into Gueliz for a haircut."

"Wish he'd come down here and distract his lordship

with blueprints for villas or whatever. What d'you think would distract that man? Tearing around the countryside after barking out orders in the morning doesn't seem to do it. Dancing girls? Wines of rare vintage?"

"I dunno. He seems to keep Digby wound up; when he's not squiring Neva around the souks it's clatter-clatter on the old Olivetti—he's on the other side of me. One thing you can say for the Hotel Elfrieda, one's never lonesome."

"You? Do you ever feel lonesome anywhere? I should doubt it." Fergus glared at her.

"I'm not about to tell you," she grinned back. "Damned if I do and damned if I don't, hmm? If you're thinking of your Aging P., all I can say is there's nothing harder than the harsh judgments of youth, babe. Tell me about your godmother."

"Cousin Elizabeth? What d'you want to hear, that she weighs twenty stone and is slightly balding, with a moustache and warts on her nose?"

"Yes."

"Too bad. She's very delightfully put together, a bit along the lines of Lady O., but taller, less breakable. A fine gardener, *femme d'interieur*, and translates Farsi, Persian. Her husband was in the Foreign Office and they were out there; she learned the language and a lot about roses as well. Gave me a prayer book and a case of port when I was born. I've mislaid the prayer book but the port should be ready to drink any day now. It used to be a whole pipe of port, but those days are gone forever. Think of it, the equivalent of two whole hogsheads. Gout guaranteed."

"Yes, then you could sit with your gouty foot elevated and play upon your pan pipes."

"Dressed in piping white with pipe clay?"

"That's a pipe dream, silly."

"Which comes from the fumes of those pipes in the

garden—come along, it's passegiata time and those groans
from the invalid—" He hunched himself up and off her
bed.

"Okay, pipe me over the side, pipsqueak."

"The angel who showed Hagar and Ishmael where the
well was in the desert could not have been fairer than
thou. Good morning." Helen took her breakfast tray from
Digby and gave him a pillow to sit on the windowsill,
crawling back into bed with her coffee. Fräulein disap-
proved of room service, and not even a "supplement"
could provide breakfast in one's rooms.

"Good morning to you. Awfully nice of you to lend
your car, Helen." He balanced delicately, half in and half
out of her room. "Let me just make a list of the things
you need. You said a London *Times?*"

"Yes . . . but only that, I just want puzzles, not news.
This one's defeating me and is pretty dog-eared anyway.
Let's see, something to keep flies off—a spray, you know.
And from a *pharmacie* something for this creeping crud
on my hands. I don't know if they're bug bites or stig-
mata, but an antibiotic cream might help." Digby looked
through the window frame at the eruptions on the backs
of her hands and wrists.

"Oh, dear, dear. I hope they're not uncomfortable?"

"Not at all, no itch or anything. Whatever the *pharmacie* has . . . expense is no object. Two bottles of scotch
and two bottles of cognac—don't blanch, that's half for
Fergus. I think that's all. Where's Stanley off to anyway?"

"Tan-Tan, I believe. He'll be back tomorrow night, as
we will."

"I wish he'd take me with him, I'd love to see what it's
like farther south. Ah, well. I'll hang in here and learn
about making soap commercials. Fergus says the tents are
coming down this afternoon, that'll be fun. Maybe shooting tomorrow, inch'allah. Here are the keys, the papers,

money, have a good trip. And thanks for the room service."

I know what a tray of ice cubes feels like when it's broken out, she thought, unloosening herself from her bed. I don't understand it—in a country where the only furniture is mattresses of one sort or another, the art of stuffing them seems to have been ignored.

"Monsieur? Madame?" Fräulein Elfrieda had dark circles under her eyes, and Helen found it difficult to ascribe the moisture on her lids to tears, but what else? Well, a confrontation with a policeman early in the morning wasn't Helen's idea of the best cosmetic; she'd passed Fräulein muttering furiously at a tall gendarme in the garden a moment before. *"Non, c'est impossible, SiSmaïl est trop malade maintenant . . . peut-être demain . . . oui, c'est dommage . . ."*

"Your passports? Ah, yes." She pulled a register out from under the bar, began making out two bills. "Passports are not returned until the bill has been paid."

"But I only want mine to cash some traveler's checks at the bank. I'm not leaving, and Lord Overton's coming back tomorrow." Helen watched the plump finger crawling across the ledger.

"It is all the same, if you wish me to keep your rooms you must pay in advance while your passports are in your possession."

"What an arrangement—no, no, Helen, put your money away, you're part of the film—Fräulein, my secretary will take care of all this, put our bills with theirs and just let me have my passport now, I'm late as it is."

"Not possible, monsieur. Your bill for number nineteen." She pushed the piece of paper across the damp bar, and Helen's to her. Stanley seized them both with irritation, leafed through his wallet, pasted notes down on the bar. Fräulein reluctantly opened a cupboard behind the

cash register, dialed at a small safe, extracted their passports, and glared at Helen. "Please be so good as to return
this when you re-enter the hotel, you have only paid until
after this morning's breakfast."

"Yass'm. B-sllama, Stanley, have a good trip." He
grunted something, brushed out through the *portiere
rideau* and Helen heard his car screech away. "Your friend
is very ill, Fräulein? Is it grave?" Elfrieda had left the door
to the safe open while she collected last night's dinner
checks from the dining room. She looked up at Helen,
slammed it shut.

"Who told you my friend was ill? It is a guest, a merchant from—Khenifra."

"Oh. I've heard whoever it is sounding uncomfortable,
that's all. Is there anything needed from Agadir? I'm sure
Mr. Marshall would be glad to bring it back."

"There is nothing." She slammed her ledgers shut, put
them under the bar, and waddled away through the passage toward the garden.

The door to Helen's room was open as she wandered
back toward the garden to wait for the bank to open; a
maid was washing the floor with a gray, sad rag. How
awful hotel rooms look in the morning, much worse than
one's own bedroom at home—why should that be? Perhaps because neatness, mopped floors, and tidy beds were
really about the only personality they had, whereas the
doodads of the years, even sickly houseplants, snapshots
in mirror frames, old letters at home seemed to lift the at-
mosphere beyond that of utility. Somehow Fräulein Elfrieda's chromos of Bavarian cows didn't quite do the job.

The windows next to her door were thrown open now
too; she looked in, hoping the moaning and groaning
stage of the invalid would soon be at an end for both
their sakes. A merchant from Khenifra, Fräulein had said.
The face on the pillow was sunken, thin, as were the
hands on the lavender plaid blanket. A green djellaba

with a woven snowflake pattern hung on a hook by the basin, and tumbled into a corner were a pair of much-worn shoes, identical to the pair Helen had bought in Tiznit. A merchant from Khenifra—the maid inside began to swing the casement windows closed, the man on the bed opened his eyes for a moment. He might be interesting to talk with if he's feeling better soon. The stubble of beard on his face and the lank hair on the pillow were dull, rough sand color, and the eyes which had stared languidly at the window for a moment before closing again were pale, watery blue.

"I don't believe it! You're in Shreveport!" Helen stood on the steps of the bank and stared at the line of people straggling off the bus.

"Oh, lordy, Helen Bullock! What are you doing down *here?* Listen, tell me quick, are you alone?" Debbysue Kemp shifted a large, ratty basket tied with cord from one shoulder to the other and gave Helen a quick pair of kisses on either cheek.

"Alone? No, not really. Not at all. I'm down here with Fergus Bede's film crew, they met you in Marrakech, and Erica's here, and the Overtons on and off—why? And what are you up to, anyway? You look wonderful." She too had picked up sun color somewhere, and her hands were elaborately decorated with henna.

"Oh, well, that's okay. Erica'll flip, but it won't be the first time. Come on, let's have a coffee at the Charazade—I hope Fräulein has a room, I've been sleeping on so many dirt floors I forget what a real bed's like."

"She's bound to. Now, tell."

"Well, I got as far as Casa, I really *did*, and spent the first day of L'Aid with some chums, but RAM really does stand for the Rottenest Airline in the Macrocosm, they'd overbooked and didn't have a seat for me or ten other people after all. So I thought what the heck, I hadn't been

down here for a long time and souk in Tiznit's on
Wednesday and I've got some *real* old friends up around
Essaouira I never got to say good-bye to"—she paused
and gave a beggar the sugar cubes from her coffee saucer
—"so I've been on and off the old buses and having a
super old time. I must say Tiznit souk's not what it used
to be, but look—" She pulled a beautiful tiny ceramic ink-
well from a bandanna in her jacket pocket, the soft turquoise and yellow glowing on the putty-colored ground.

"Lovely. What is that sticking out of your basket—is
that all you have with you?"

"Yep, everything else is with my buddies in Casa. That
thing, oh, I hope it survives till I get home—it's a gorgeous
butter churn, weighs a ton, some kind of stoneware, but
the glaze is this heavenly green, see?"

"Heavenly. Deb, you might not have heard—have you
see anyone from Marrakech, from the Center?"

"—do wait until tomorrow. For one thing, your replacement should be there by now, Stanley got that going with
the people in Rabat."

"Oh, but then they'll need me even more, he won't
know *anything*—"

"Don't you think your rushing back now might be a bit
unfair to this new guy? He's got to start sometime."

Debbysue blew her nose and hiccuped with tears. "But
I wouldn't be interfering, you know, it's just that—"

"He'd think you were. Honey, do wait a few days. Telephone, sure, but remember those little boys aren't dumb,
they'll probably want to help him, don't you think? If you
were there it'd be a tug at their loyalties."

"Yeah, you're right. Thanks. Poor Abdellatif, though.
Poor old SiOmar, too. He must feel awful." She stared,
unseeing, at Philip and Maurice unlocking the vans, load-
ing in camera cases. "And poor Kauder."

"Kauder?"

"Oh, you wouldn't have known, I forgot. He wasn't ashamed of the boy—that's what his Arabic name meant, you know, Ali Ben Abdellatif—Ali, son of the Latvian, like a nickname—lots of unintended babies around—no shame for the man, and the mother's dead a long time. It was just easier for him to have Latif live there like the real orphans, he'd been there since he was four. So there's only his father, Kauder."

Of course, Helen thought. That's what Erica had meant when she soothed Arthur, "There'd be no point . . . now that it's all over . . ."

CHAPTER VIII

"So," Helen wrote on the notebook propped on her knee, "we sit here in the expensive party tents by the oasis, prisoners of a sandstorm, which began blowing up appropriately just after noon. Appropriately, because for some reason Fräulein sent out fifty ham sandwiches for lunch, perfectly all right for us pig eaters, but the Sepoy Rebellion isn't in it as far as the shaykh (who honors us with his presence at lunch every day) and the khalifa and *guardiens* and the cadre of blue men we are supposed to feed. What was in that woman's mind, and where indeed did she find ham in such a place?

"The blue men—more grimy gray than blue, but Erica will fix that, I'm sure—saw to their camels and then had themselves driven back to Goulimine in high dudgeon (a euphemism for the truck in which they travel); I think they knew the storm was coming and that we wouldn't be working anyway." She looked up from her letter to Simon. Philip and Maurice were playing mumblety-peg in a dim corner of the tent; Fergus was lying on his stomach looking out a slit in the canvas at the hissing sand; Sherif was rolled in his djellaba next to her, asleep. She brushed the lace of flies from his eyelids, wondering how anyone escaped trachoma here.

"The new ramparts are splendid, and Fergus happy about the shooting to date—a predictable number of takes marred by a stray donkey, an errant cloud, the horses meant to keep the camels in line getting into the frame, but he's wondrously patient; there's one last charge from the gate to get in the can, and he's promised me I can put on a big turban and if I don't giggle visibly can join the gang on a camel in the background; Sherif is *désolée* since he is really too short, but he does have the overseerage of ten boys with palm fronds who sweep the sand after every take. Is he taking kickbacks from their two dirhams apiece a day? This we do not know exactly, but he's having a great time.

"Stanley is continuing to tear around the countryside when he isn't driving Fergus up the wall with gratuitous suggestions; if he's looking for hotel sites he's going to some very dry places unless he plans to fill the swimming pools with Jell-O. There's an idea . . . strawberry trampolines. Neva has been out here twice, finds it too dusty, and plays Penelope at the hotel with her needlepoint.

"Debbysue has bewitched the khalifa, who now breathes heavily when either Erica or she appears. He's a nice young man, I think he was hoping for platinum movie stars, etc. (how d'you like this, by the way: breast sing.: *bzoola*, plural: *bzazzle*? It's true), but is wielding governmental authority gracefully and has kept the price down on the whole thing, wages and ramparts, and the fear of Allah in one and all about being late, etc. Have decided one reason all seem grumpy is living off tea and bread and sugar—I avoid it as best I can but I think it's getting to me at this point."

The wind hissed unrelentingly outside, the camels and horses and donkeys groaned resignedly; this was nothing to them, nothing at all. Men from the village lay in the tents, their turbans as pillows, dreaming, sleeping, the wind blew, the sand blew, it would stop when it stopped.

"Debbysue and Erica took off for the village when Fergus downed tools—they'd spotted a woman wearing a pair of silver anklets and by this time I'm sure the girls own them or they've been murdered. DS will have enough objects to open a museum in Shreveport if she ever gets home . . . I wish I dared ask her why she dallies so. Knowing myself, I probably will. She's a great haggler, and helped me buy an 'antique' silver water bottle one of the village men brought around. As proof of its authenticity he showed me the 'ancient' coins set in among the arabesques and engravings, not quite '212 B.C.' but one of them is, very charmingly, one of your English slot machine tokens (which he told me was a Portuguese escudo). I like the shape of the bottle, and it was fun. The camel bag, by the way, has a very ethnic smell now that it's in my hotel room—perhaps it will wear off."

She yawned, doodled a less than successful henna design on her hand with her pen, admired her rings, examined the welts or bites or whatever they were. Fergus stirred, rolled over. "Okay, team, this is enough, even if the wind stops now the light'll be gone. Sherif, run get the girls from the village, okay? Where's Khalifa Rachid? Oh, yes, if you can get the *guardiens* organized now— they'll sleep here in the tents? Good—we can call it a day."

"This beats anything Neva's likely to have found in Agadir. For twenty-five cents it's a steal." Helen sat on the slimy cement floor of the hammam, between Erica and Debbysue, and looked about her. It seemed, in the dim light, that someone had delivered a load of white eggplants, albino zucchinis, long curving squashes, and round gourds, all pale, translucent, tumbled on the steamy floor together. Yes, fat was definitely in, it seemed opulent rather than indulgent. These ladies all had wrists and waists and ankles, not the stocky shoulder to knee heft of overweight Europeans.

"Yes, but it's really not fair, women have to pay more than men because we use more water on our hair, and then they say we stay longer just to talk. Erica, lend me some shampoo, honey? Well, I ask you, women haven't got anyplace else to get together, they sure can't sit around in the cafés going yackety-yack. I tell you, it's a man's world." Debbysue poured a bucket of hot water over herself exuberantly. "Oh, does that feel good!"

Helen, sweating gloriously, was scrubbing Erica's back with a piece of wood covered with crocheted string; what seemed like the dead skin of centuries had come off her own back with the thing; Erica's was glowing pink now.

"Can you imagine Neva in here? It'd be like a Meissen shepherdess in a dishwasher." Helen laughed at her own question. All these naked women lying about, splashing, gossiping, rinsing henna from their hair, slapping and scrubbing their children; the hot water steaming from a well like an inferno; two scrawny women, bath attendants who would scrub one for a price, tugging wooden buckets across the floor with stringy arms, their flaccid empty breasts dangling uselessly.

"No, even in my wildest fancy I cannot imagine Neva here." Erica smiled over her shoulder. "I don't think I've ever seen her perspire, much less sweat. They do have a super sauna in London, but that's surely for Stanley. Ah, well, some of us have all the luck, and some don't. All that Wilcox money—you don't know, Deb, but Neva's just come into almost a million pounds on her own, an old aunt she lived with before she married—finally kicked the bucket last month. And there's only little Neva to inherit —it's really more than one can bear. Well, there's some bother with the will or something, but it's only a question of time, not fact. Now she's not only rich, but independently rich. I am green."

"Me, I'm independently poor. I agree, a million anything would be very nice indeed. Oh my lord, look—" Helen grabbed Debbysue's wet knee and put a hand over her mouth; a vast lady had come in and pulled her water buckets over, sat down next to them. On one plump wrist a large, handsome wristwatch had been tattooed in rich blue, the time shown was ten minutes to six.

"How long does henna last, like on your hands and feet, Debbysue?"

"Oh, a couple of weeks usually." She spread out her hands and looked at them. "I guess I'd better get started home if I want to show it to Daddy before it wears off. Now listen, Erica, what did you mean back in Marrakech telling Neva—when we were all having lunch at your house—you'd only been up to London overnight? You were gone a week—nice old hanky-panky, I hope?"

"My dear girl"—Erica smiled at her with lazy eyes, lathering her skin with a soft flannel cloth—"you don't expect me to tell, do you? No, that's not fair—I like Neva, but she does expect ladies in waiting, and I had a lot of business to do; I didn't look them up until the day before I left. Actually, just Stanley, he lent me a lawyer. That is very *entre nous*. You had your henna done in the wilds, didn't you?"

"Yeah, it's pretty simple, but it still took six hours, and do I hate sleeping with it all wrapped up overnight. Well, maybe I'll make my fortune by inventing instant . . . decals, or something." Debbysue stood up and poured buckets of water over their three foaming, sudsy heads.

Revitalized and virtually steaming, their wet towels and dirty clothes in a basket, they strode across the dark square and through the passage from the hotel's bar to the garden archway. "Oh my *golly!*" Debbysue pulled Helen back under the arch and blocked Erica's way. "Oh, jeepers, what'll I do? Helen, you've got to hide me—Erica, promise you won't say a word, I'll sneak off on the bus first thing in the morning, I swear I will—*What* is he doing here?"

Stanley sat with his back to them at a table halfway down the garden, with a freshly coiffed Neva and three of Fräulein's expensive whiskeys on the table; both the

Overtons were laughing at something the third person was saying, his dark, glossy good looks and air of authority recognizable across the little crocheted caps on the heads of the kif smokers, the beer drinkers. Mustapha Jouti was telling what seemed to be a very funny story.

"I should have known," Debbysue brooded as she and Helen bumped their way along the *piste* leading to Ait Bouchka the next morning. "He and Stanley are thick as thieves and he'd be bound to show up. Poor old thing, when he thought he'd gotten me out of his hair for good."

"How'd he get here? He said something about his car not being here until this morning." Helen swerved quickly, avoiding a dubious patch of thick sand in the road and jouncing them over rocks instead.

"Flew to Sidi Ifni, it's the closest airstrip. I suppose the governor sent him over last night. Oh, well, just as long as he doesn't think I'm chasing after him and cramping his style. Hey, you know, that Khalifa Rachid's a real cute guy, he looks a lot like young Jimmy Carter must have, don't you think?"

Come to think of it, Helen mused as she drove up next to the vans, he does a little bit, especially in jeans and the Polaroid sunglasses Stanley had given him. Nice big white teeth and the same kind of hair. He and the crew were standing by the folding aluminum script table, the sparkling black-and-white tents in the background with the herd of camels and horses beyond.

"Well, that just about tears it." Fergus picked a clipboard off the table and sailed it like a paper-laden Frisbee out toward the oasis behind the tents. Helen thought she'd never seen anything as black as his face. At a hiss from Rachid, Sherif went running after the board and Fergus stormed into the nearest tent. Erica shrugged, pulled the scarf off her hair and came up to Helen and

Debbysue. She leaned against the side of a van and sighed.

"We'd better leave him alone for a moment, he's having his first taste of just *how* bloody minded this country can be. It all began with those ham sandwiches yesterday —remember the blue men went back in the trucks in a huff? Well, they're not here this morning; Sherif says he saw them all in the men's hammam last night, sweating and soaking out of pique about the ham—wouldn't believe it was all a terrible mistake—and consequently all the blue is gone, gone, gone from their dratted skins."

"Poor Fergus." Helen looked at the sky, it was a clear sapphire yet once more, but how long would it last?

"Rachid's going over to the next douar—they won't be far away as long as their camels are here; he'll bring them back by noon one way or another, inch'allah. But one of the *guardiens* let a goat get into the prop tent after we left yesterday, and it ate up the very last cake of soap, the one Fergus needs for the close-up. Paper and all."

"Oh, jeepers." Debbysue gave Sherif a pat and took the clipboard from him.

"Yes, but the final blow—we can fake the blue on the men somehow when they come back—I don't know about the soap—the final blow is that the beasts ate the ham sandwiches the men threw away, and as a consequence every last camel has diarrhea."

"Patience, old boy," Helen could hear Stanley rumbling away to Fergus at the table outside her window. "These things happen, have another brandy now, do." Coals to Newcastle, Helen thought, working away at the project spread out on her bed—involving razor blades, glue, tape, the carton her scotch had come in, black Pentels. Fergus was tight as a tick already, and a good thing for him it was. He'd sleep it off and be fit as a flea tomorrow. Stanley, however, needed catching up. Jouti'd taken the

Overtons and Helen to the pasha's house for dinner; the soft drinks and tea had flowed like wine during the interminable meal.

Neva was playing bridge with Jouti, Erica, and Maurice. Rachid had come around after dinner and taken Debbysue and Philip off to a party at someone's house, they'd wheedled a key from the watchman and wouldn't be back until two or three, Deb had been sure. "It'll be ya-ya-ya-luv-luv-luv singing and tea-tea-tea drinking and I'll have a sugar hangover for sure in the morning, but I can't resist."

Surveying her handiwork, Helen applied a third and final coat of Erica's hair spray to it and waved the fumes away. Not bad at all—if it only looked as well in the harsh light of the sun it'd cheer Fergus up no end. She must tell him that she'd decided that if everything depended on inch'allah, God's will, then today was one of the things she'd determined was an outch'allah, and *not* meant to happen. Or at least not the way one had planned it.

As she came out of her room Fräulein herself was marching through the arch holding a minuscule teapot and one glass on a tray. Must be for the sick merchant— nobody else gets any sort of room service except via dear Digby. What's he up to? Oh, there he was, doing some sort of sums on a pocket calculator at Stanley's table. "You're almost three quid ahead, Lady Overton." Neva nodded happily, shuffled, dealt, her rings flashing up at the enormous stars shimmering through the vine.

Sudden crashing sundered the peace under the palmettos and hibiscus, a bull-like roaring of anger came from something that wore white and was crashing about. Fräulein put the tray down abruptly on the table between Stanley and Fergus and began to shriek to the bar for the waiter, scurried back through the arch and returned in a moment with a terrified watchman swinging a massive

wooden cudgel, she herself clutching an enormous shotgun designed to kill, at the very least, condors, if not rocs.
Beating her way past the upright bridge players, she burrowed into the underbrush, the watchman on one side,
and between they dragged out a scuffling, fist-swinging,
bellicose drunk whose eyes rolling back in his head and
his turban falling awry didn't for a moment keep him
from swinging viciously at Digby, at Fräulein, at Helen,
who scurried aside.

"I say, I say—" Stanley pushed his way forward, but
Fräulein turned the man's right arm over to Fergus, who
got it in a hammerlock while she proceeded to blister his
face with slaps from one hand while the other jabbed him
in the belly with the butt of the gun, and not gingerly.
Nor was the resulting blast of the shotgun gingerly, the
pellets fortunately exploding into the dank shrubbery, but
a few skidded around Helen's and Digby's ankles. Neva
screamed, somehow the game table was knocked over,
glasses and cards strewn among the toppled chairs. The
watchman skulked in the shadows. Jouti shielded Neva
while Fergus tried to pull the now-tearful and sobbing
drunk away from Fräulein, and Erica and Maurice tried
to pull Fräulein away from the wretch.

Twenty minutes later the garden was tidied, quiet;
Stanley had tucked Neva in bed with a sleeping pill, had
come out with a bottle of them for anyone who wanted
one, recommending they all turn in as well. Fräulein had
sent a waiter back to them after the stowaway had been
ejected; he had explained the man was an old uncle of
someone important, thus was allowed to enter Fräulein's
with the afternoon clientele, had done this before—fallen
asleep in the bushes from too much beer, too much kif; all
was well, no harm was done, the shotgun was of course
only for such emergencies. Would anyone be wanting
anything, or could he close the bar now? Fräulein pushed
through the arch, head belligerently down and the palm

of her hand still red from the raging slaps; she collected
the little teapot on the tray and had gone into number 8
without a nod or glance or apology.

Helen woke in the dark of the night, vertically and immediately awake, and swore furiously. If one of her classic patches of waking from three to six had begun, there
was little she could do about it, but this wasn't the most
amusing place to be smitten. Life began early here, she'd
be bleary-eyed and tired during the most interesting parts
of the day, and there weren't any all-night movies to
watch on the television she didn't have. Working on her
puzzle would be fatal, it would only wake her up even
more. How ridiculous they were. Old Captain keeps Erica
dry. 8. That had been MacHeath, after four days of noo-
dling.

The dial of her watch showed four-ten. Oh Gawd. Now
I won't get back to sleep until six-thirty, but if I take a
sleeping pill now it'll be disaster in the morning and we're
shooting the last camel charge, Fergus promised I could
be in it. Relax, relax, imagine somebody massaging the
back of your neck, your shoulders. No good. And no electricity. Fräulein's thrift seemed to have cut it off at some
point. She lit the stump of candle by her bed.

Shivering as she looked at herself in the flickering light
reflected in the greenish mirror over the washbasin, she
pulled a sweater over her nightgown, flopped back in bed
and punched up the pillows. How bitchy I've been to
Simon, I shouldn't have run off from Crumbles like that,
really. Well, yes, I should have, because after all Arthur
and I go back a long, long way. But I needn't have
stayed; he's not exactly at death's door, and a fat lot of
good I'm doing him here. Not quite true, Stanley and
Jouti had been full of enthusiasm about "the Bettman
touch" at dinner tonight, vis-à-vis a hotel on the beach at
Tan-Tan, and there was that memo Stanley had written

to himself on the list of little towns about the Todra Gorge—something about being careful of shadows, use skylights, something. But after all—where should she be? Where do I want to be? New York? Crumbles? Here? Asleep, that's what I want.

Something rustled among the plants outside her open window, a rooster crowed in the distance, the tap in her washbasin dripped. Then she heard a low, heavy groan, and something smothered, a sound between a shout and a scream. The invalid next door sounded absolutely in extremis. She pulled on socks—damn, she'd never remember to give them to Fergus—took her candle and wondered where in hell she'd find Fräulein. Did the maids sleep in the hotel? The waiters? The watchman should be out in the parking area. Everything was locked, there was no one, no one. She paused for a moment outside number 8, the agony of sound was real and she opened the door and hurried in.

The man had fallen to the cold floor, was lying on his side with an edge of sheet clasped in his fist, the other hand beating weakly on the tiles, the deep rasping wails taking all his strength so that the hoarse whispers between spasms were weak seedlings in a forest of pain. The room stank of vomit, alcohol; the bed was stained with it and splotches of blood dappled the sheet under the man's head. Helen bent down beside him, tried to ask him what to do, felt his ice-cold cheek, hand, as a great spasm of nausea buckled him in an arc. A river of blood burst from his open, howling mouth and shot across the floor, subsiding as she knelt in terror and watched him die.

"Who gave SiSmaïl the brandy? Who?" Fräulein Elfrieda in her heliotrope nightgown and purple black hair looked like a death's head in Day-Glo colors, her face gray with fury as she slapped maids, hit waiters, the barman trying to calm her as she punched him in the belly with an empty brandy bottle stained in blood from the man's hemorrhage. The dining room's lights were relentless, leaving none of her grossness imagined, nor any of her rage. "One of you must have given it to Smaïl, I will find out if I have to pull out your fingernails one by one—"

Joyeux Noël, the dusty ribbons strung from the ceiling quivered, the maids cried and the men cringed.

"My dear Fräulein." Stanley, his hair ruffled and eyes bleary, stood in a maroon silk kimono in the doorway.

"Milord!" she turned to him. "I must call the police, have the gendarmes take these criminals to the prison, my old friend SiSmaïl is lying dead in his room because one of them gave him a bottle of brandy, he was very ill you understand with the *foie, il était très, très malade, gràve vous comprenez, avec la hepatite virale. Pour lui donner une bouteille de cognac—*" The waiters, who understood French, began further protestations, head-shaking negations for themselves and translations for the two maids.

"Good Lord! Why didn't he tell me? Fräulein, I implore you, calm yourself." Stanley sat down suddenly and banged a fist on a table. "The silly ass—I knew him very slightly, Fräulein, from many years ago, didn't know he was here at all until I happened to see him through his window this morning. He was asleep. Tonight—tonight, it must have been about two, I got up to go to the loo, his light was on, his candle—he called to me as I went by, said hello, asked if I had any drink, would I come in for a chat. I brought some cognac from my room, he wanted to apologize about leaving the film, this and that. Afraid I dropped a brick, he hadn't heard about his son at the Center. Awful shock, he took quite a bit of cognac, finally seemed sleepy and I left. I never dreamed—he didn't seem ill, looked older, but then we all do, there was only the candle—" Stanley's French abandoned him. He turned to Helen. "Is he really dead?"

She nodded, twisting the hem of her sweater, which

was stained with blood. She saw the red on her hand, her nightgown, socks.

"The fool, the damn old fool—you say he had hepatitis? My God, drink's like arsenic for that, what was he thinking of? He had several—the bottle was half empty when I left it with him."

Elfrieda had collapsed like an unsatisfactory pudding. She looked up piteously from the chair where her haunches overflowed. "I cannot believe he was such a fool—he had had this before, it is *partout,* the hepatitis in this country, he was very careful, each time it was more grave, his liver was not good anymore—"

Helen had found the brandy bottle when they lifted his body back onto the bed—it was on the floor beneath him. She had unthinkingly put it on the table with the little teapot, glass, candle, and an old grimy paperback of *Shogun,* tattered and with the binding coming apart. Still life, she'd thought, *nature morte.*

"Ah, I do not believe you, *c'est impossible,*" Fräulein screamed at Stanley suddenly, "he was on a journey of much urgency to Tarfaya but became ill here, he knew to take nothing, nothing but water, a *tisane* for sleeping— I myself put laudanum in his *tisane* each night—I would not let the gendarme tell him about the boy until he was better . . ."

"*Madame, vous m'excuse.*" Helen indicated her bloody nightwear, her hands, turned to the door. Stanley opened it for her, his face drawn, pale. "Is there anything we should do, Stanley, the police or a doctor—who *was* he, you said you knew him? Smaïl something?"

"Oh, that's the name he uses—used with the locals, easier for them and polite as well, I suppose—he thought it a bit of a joke for some reason. Sorry, I thought you'd met." The hollow tones of a cocktail party whispered among the Christmas ribbons. "It's Kauder, of course, Gleb Kauder."

CHAPTER IX

The rain seemed pettish, grudging, doing nothing any good. Not the tiny farms with their one short season for salvation, nor the dusty streets of Goulimine, and only chilling the already cold body that was being loaded into an army truck for the drive back to Marrakech and the cemetery for Europeans.

Digby was putting the Overtons' luggage into the Mercedes, looking very "towny" in his Burberry and muffler. Helen came out to say good-bye to him, he pulled the envelope with her shopping list written on it and gave it to her. "Your change, I'm dreadfully sorry I forgot." There was a careful accounting listed on it, the dear man.

"Drive carefully, and see you back in Marrakech I hope. No, no tomobil today, Sherif." The boy couldn't really have expected it, with the pewter skies, but since for him there was only hope, hope he would.

Stanley was in the dining room, urging Neva to have more tea, eat something, before they set out, it would be a long day; the pasha himself came in with Rachid, suitably dressed in a sober djellaba. Important regrets were exchanged, assurances of support, a terrible contretemps, but anyone, anyone at all under the same conditions—if there were any occasion to be of help in the future—

"Morning, Ferg." The not-so-bright and very sad waiter brought Helen coffee, fresh bread, canned milk.

"How are you, lady? Get any sleep at all? I gather it was quite a night."

"Enough, I suppose. It was. No film today, of course?"

"No, no film today. Well, sir, this is an unhappy ending to a fine beginning; I hope you have a bearable trip." Fergus stood up, holding his napkin, as Overton shook hands with them.

"Thank you. Helen, I hope to see you back in Marrakech. Bede, it shouldn't take more than a day or so down here, the pasha swears the rain's blowing over already. Perhaps we should scratch this one after all, a bit recherché if you ask me, blue men. Jouti'll be here for a day or so, business in Ifni, if you have any problems. Good luck."

"Recherché." Fergus groaned and put his head in his hands. "After tearing everything to bits and hauling us down here and building ramparts—oh God. I hope to heaven old Kauder didn't know, not even that we were here. Not that *he'd* have minded, it was all the same to him."

Helen, hugging herself against the cold, mooched into the garden and saw the door of Kauder's room open, a maid with a bucket flinging horribly pink water onto the hibiscus and oleanders. She gathered up the stained nightwear in her room and put it on the floor under her washbasin—Fräulein did not run to wastebaskets. They would wash, but she somehow didn't want them anymore. Nor did she want to sleep in this room again. Perhaps she'd change to Neva's, it should feel safe and snug in its corner. No, it was just dank, dark, not really amusing enough with the velour hanging of the dogs playing poker to offset the gloom. Her tea tray looked chill and sad on the little plastic table; she'd tossed a silk scarf with a tiny hole in it into the corner, an empty perfume spray, a copy of *Elle*, makeup, stained Kleenex.

Number 19, Stanley's, was infinitely better with the fake chimney front and the lions in cut velvet, and the huge bathtub beyond the bedroom. That would be heaven in the heat of July, except of course the water tank would

very likely be on the roof and thus the water would be as
unbearably hot then as it was cold now. Stanley couldn't
steam out his suits here; perhaps Digby had a little traveling iron. She lay down on the tumbled sheets; yes, the
bed felt better than her own, much better. And there was
actually a little table high enough to write on without
doubling over, a chair instead of the ubiquitous low
stools. And, mirabile dictu, a wastebasket! *Quelle luxe.*

The second maid put her gaily scarfed head with its
mournful face through the window, looking startled at
Helen occupying milord's bed, and moved on toward
Neva's rooms. She sat up. What a mess even the most elegant people produce as they move through the world;
Stanley's trash was neatly contained in the basket, but
still, trash—an empty tube of hair cream, pipe tobacco
tins, a disposable razor, an empty bottle of scotch, crumpled pharmacist's paper from Agadir, colored postcards.
She reached down for those—they looked unused, and she
should send Simon one, and Arthur too. Snake charmers,
just the thing. She pulled a blanket up, sat back against
the bolsters.

Not postcards, photographs. No, photograms, no doubt
printed in London from the film Fergus sent up every
week; the minutely altered position of the cobra's head
and hood, the flutist's hands showed that. The process itself of printing a still from a frame of film was as familiar
to Helen as her own feet. This must be the spot Stanley'd
wanted reshot in an interior, then, the one Fergus
growled about. Well, there were a lot of people standing
about, looking a bit silly and touristy, but that was authentic after all. How many snake charmers sat around
without an audience, tootling a flute and exhausting their
reptiles just for the fun of it? Not many, she thought.
Maybe it was too authentic, though. The flutist's partner
was playing a viola, for one thing, and the wooden box
that had the bloated adder dripping over the side did

look like a carpenter's tool kit. She looked closer. Mingling with the tourists, half hidden and somewhat bored looking, was a man in a djellaba with a snowflake pattern, the hood hiding half his face, but even so, Helen could see it was Kauder.

"Hey there." Debbysue poked her head through the window. "What're you *doing?*"

"Trying to see if some of his lordship's classiness will rub off on me, I guess." Helen pulled the blanket over her head.

"Pooh, you need class like I need a third *bzoola.*" Debbysue reached in, pulled it down. "Bad day, though, isn't it, we're all feeling terrible—you'd never met him, but you'll have to help get us through the gloom. He was kind of nice, the kind of man my mama would say about 'there's no knot in his thread,' but nice. Anyway, Jouti's taking us all to lunch over in Sidi Ifni, he called the hotel and it's nice and sunny and it'll cheer us all up, the sea and the beach, so can we take your car too? I'm all packed. Jouti's going to have his plane fly me up to Casa after lunch, isn't that sweet?"

"Sure, if you want to go. You can always ride back to Marrakech with me, you know. We'll miss you."

"Oh, me too, but Jouti's got RAM over the ropes *and* barbed wire about that booking, you've never heard anybody burn up the telephone like he did. So they have a seat for me tomorrow. Come on, you can help wave me off in style."

"Stanley darling, you mustn't feel dreadful about all this, how could you have known? I'd never even met him, and you certainly didn't know him well."

"Still, such a rotten way for a fellow to go, must have been sheer hell from what Helen said." Stanley patted Neva's hand, watched the flat dull land unroll outside the car window, the flat dull back of Digby's head.

"I should think she was being a bit—exaggerated. Now you said you'd always tried to help him when you could—"

"That wasn't bloody often, I can tell you. I only ran into him four or five times since the war."

"But when you did, when you could—it's not your fault if he wasn't around very often? And do remember he was the one who upped and left the film on the spur of the moment—very inconsiderate. Frankly, I'm going to be realistic and say it doesn't sound like he's a terrible loss to the world in terms of other people, and it seems he lived exactly as he chose to, which is a great deal more than most of us can do."

"All right, sweet. As you say. Are you sure you don't want to stop the night in Agadir, or go back by way of Essaouira for something of a change? That hotel was a bit much for you—there's a splendid new one there you haven't seen and might enjoy."

"No, it's always so windy and cold there. Let's go straight on home—if Marrakech is going to be home."

It was indeed a fine day in Sidi Ifni, and Sidi Ifni needed all the help it could get in spite of the elegant crescent of beach curving whitely below the Hotel Beauregard on its high cliff. The Spanish had left almost two decades ago, grudgingly; their empty villas, the promenade, and the escalier descending to the beach crumbling now, the streets empty of even blowing newspapers. Time had not stood still, it had hurried, hurried to turn the bit of hated Spain into a ghost town, the casino empty on the beach, broken glass in windows, the church without bell or cross and the paint on the villas turned the color of old canceled checks.

Jouti had driven Debbysue and Helen hell for leather over the dry, scrubby mountains, oblivious of goats, children, women, scattering them behind him on the roadside; the official green plates of a Minister of State caused a police block to drop its barrier just in time. "Smugglers, always a problem here," he had explained blithely. Debbysue seemed to be accustomed to the pace, and dozed in the back seat, her bright hair pillowed on the shredding butter-churn basket.

"Tarfaya? Very far down in the south, on the sea. He had many friends there, I think, or perhaps Tan-Tan, Gleb. Lazy? You must not forget we see these things differently. To you, to Overton—I have discovered you are very accomplished, Helen, famous indeed—yes, you would think him lazy perhaps. To our farmers, our nomads in the *bled,* the countryside, a useful man with machinery, radios, generous, perhaps a bit of a mystic? This we do not know exactly. Many strange people come here, you know; unlike hippies he was welcome I think."

"He came here in the war?"

"Yes, yes. A French passport, Free French, he had no problem staying on. A good *mechanicien,* very needed then with windmills, broken-down buses, generators for electricity; by the time there was need he had learned our languages perfectly and could earn well, driving and guiding scholars, expeditions in the desert. And you know of el Glaoui? Of course. Gleb was given that house in Marrakech by that monster, he had a passion for model trains but no . . . no expertise himself. Kauder could repair anything, the pasha's clocks as well, his golf cart, many things. After el Glaoui died he was not obliged to be in the city, but kept the house for selling things he had found in the country when he needed money. His friends from the mountains, from here, would bring in things, he would help them find buyers—his life did not need much money, he was always a country person."

"Do many people 'go native' here?"

"None. It is not possible. My people know everything, they talk, they gossip, everyone knows who is who. He wore djellaba, of course, for comfort, used the name Smaïl because it was easier for his friends just as Erica is Rhykia to her workers—so many of my people are backward, backward. There is a word for people like Kauder, I cannot think of it in English—it has to do with hair—"

"Hair? I wonder what it is. How'd Stanley know him?"

"The *prison militaire* in Ifni—ah, there it is ahead"—a strip of flat blue sea twinkled in the sun—"Kauder stayed on here, his own country had Russians." Had Russians, Helen thought, like smallpox. A good way to put it. "Many did, I am told, it was all much confused, different borders, fewer roads, it is much better today, L'Hamdullah."

The hotel had turned its back in its death throes to the sea; the terrace with the lighthouse was now only for parking—parking cars that did not come. A stench of death permeated the place, only from cracked and rotten drains, but Helen was glad to follow Debbysue back outside onto the balcony of the bar, overlooking a small green square. Jouti had left them to go find a waiter, service; they could hear his voice echoing arrogantly in the long empty halls inside. It was all very, very out of a movie where The Bomb had dropped and they were the last three survivors.

Except for the young peacocks in their cheap pointed-toed shoes, Italianate haircuts, tight trousers, drinking beer at the next table. They laughed at a remark one made; he repeated it rather loudly as Jouti appeared with a waiter. He turned on them, a scorching vitriolic stream hissed out, and the trio abashedly slunk off in single file, one of them defiantly carrying his beer with him.

"You must excuse such young—punks, is the word? The shame of my country, this drinking, drinking by the young. If you will tell the *garçon*— I must see the kitchen—" Jouti went back inside.

"What'd those boys say, Deb?"

"Oh, the usual cracks about sex-starved foreign ladies and virile Moroccan men. Water off a duck's back to me, but you can see how he'd mind. Hi there, you all had a good ride?" Helen's car, with Fergus and Erica, pulled up by the square. They waved, ordered from the waiter, and Helen hoped that whatever was going to be served for lunch wouldn't be permeated by the stench inside.

"You must have," Fergus rumbled, pulling out a chair for Erica and taking a swig of Helen's beer. "Fast, at least. Your car is very Mickey Mouse."

"I know, but it's fun. Erica, what a treat you are to look at, good for you." She had left her country working clothes in Goulimine, and looked the talented designer she was, dark green wool whitening her skin and the seams woven together in indigo and magenta floss.

"You like?" she asked to Helen's avidly approving look. "I'll do you one when we get back—I would have shown you this before, but I'd run out of the sabra—the floss. I have it dyed just for me in Fès, it's my trademark. There should be some at home by now, though. When are you thinking of finishing, Fergus?"

"If Philip and Maurice are doing their stuff today with that camera that keeps jamming, and Rachid gets the camels over the collywobbles, two days? If nothing else goes wrong."

"Ah, nothing will go wrong"—Jouti sat down, snapped his fingers for the waiter to serve a bottle of wine—"no gloom now, we have a nice luncheon and when we get back to Goulimine there will be no clouds at all. Of any kind. Inch'allah."

But in spite of the sun on the sea, their party clothes after days of dust and dungarees, the wine and food, there was an air of restriction, failure of resilience about them all; Helen could only smile tiredly at Jouti when he said, "I have just remembered that word, a beachbrusher. No? Ah, yes, beachcomber. Yes, he was beachcomber."

And the champagne that was brought out for a farewell toast to Debbysue was not cold, and it was very flat.

The little airplane, polished and very expensive-looking, was waiting at the airstrip the Spanish had been unable to take away with them. Jouti's pilot waited outside the small cabin on the pavement, hoping he could have the night in Casablanca rather than flying back down here today, this was a dull place, Ifni.

"Now, little darling"—Jouti was fastening Debbysue's seat belt; he had stowed her distressing basket under the second seat—"so sad, but much much more comfortable than driving back to Marrakech with Helen, *wakha?* My office will have your ticket at the airport; this time there will be no dreadful problems and you will not have to wander around the countryside. Now please close your beautiful eyes."

She opened them on a wonder of small pearls in a thick ropy festoon around her neck, a fortune clasped on each side by gold bosses with pale green stones, the luminous pearls the dream of every woman here. The many strands were as thick as her wrist and long enough to fall to her breasts. "Oh, darling, no, no, you've given me far too much—" He shut her soft, plump mouth with his hand, kissed her eyes closed again, jumped down from the cabin and curtly told the pilot for God's sake to take off and get her to Casablanca without fail, and to see that she got on the plane to America in the morning and stayed on it if he had to kill her to do it.

Turning, he smoothed his silky hair back and strode to the group waiting by their cars. Ah, yes, the decks were cleared for so many things now; now Kauder's house would be free and make the bijou little hotel in the medina a certain success; the others, with Stanley, would, of course, make money, but this little one—this would have cachet. A pity about the pearls, he'd brought them down

from Rabat for Erica. Still, he couldn't send little Debbysue off with nothing, and there were more pearls. Perhaps it would be prudent, more tasteful, to begin with a
long weekend in Paris or London with Erica at Noël; she
would probably like that very much. His eyes gleamed at
the sight of her, the copper hair blowing in the wind and
a cool smile on her lips.

"Fergus, I think Allah's put his finger on you." Helen,
divested of the disguising turban she had worn among the
ranks of the blue riders, but enjoying the yardage of her
own blue draa against the hot midday sun, smeared blue
ink from the palm of her hand onto her upper lip as she
wiped sweat away. Four perfect camel charges from the
fort and ramparts were in the can, it was only noon, and
all that was left to be done—since Fergus had no interest
in using the silly tents at all—was the close-up of the most
personable and authentic blue man discovering the soap,
with the oasis in the background.

"Oh Lord, I hope so. Rachid, can you get the camels
organized and somewhere out of the way—we don't want
one running astray into the shot; and where's that Daki
we chose yesterday? Time for his close-up, no lunch for
anyone until it's done. Beef today, by the way."

Rachid was slowly overcoming his dislike at being
jounced about the countryside and placating surly camel
men and greedy shaykhs. A camaraderie of difficulty, and
a camaraderie of success, had developed; this young man
Bede seemed never in a hurry, seldom cross or disap-
pointed as so many foreigners did. And although there
was no gold-and-white movie star, this lady Erica underneath her dark scarf and plain clothes—how sad, he could
see no more of her than of his own sisters—was someone
to look up when he was in Marrakech.

And that woman who seemed to have nothing much to

do with anything, she had made Fergus very happy by making a cardboard box and drawing a wrapper for it just as before, exactly like the box the goat had eaten, so there was something to be photographed on the brass tea tray that *disgusting* Daki, who was supposed to wash the blue off his hands and face, could take up. How insane, when had Daki ever washed to begin with, they were all filthy, and who would have a fine brass seâia down here? Crazy, all of it, but interesting.

"Yes, the ink is really better than their own grotty blue, you know, Fergus." Erica tossed an empty bottle of Waterman's washable blue to the ground, opened another. "I'm sure you'll be far happier with this." She began repairing the color on Daki's face, his sweat was making it run and he looked a bit like a blue zebra.

"You're likely right. Now, Rachid, are you absolutely certain he understands he's *not* to *open* the package in this take? Just reach for it, pick it up, hold it up with a smile with the tips of his fingers—like this?" Fergus went through the exact motions he wanted as Rachid began translating for the third time; Daki nodded solemnly as Erica rearranged the folds of his draa to make his shoulders look even broader. "It's our only package, soap cakes for the final shot we've got lots of, Palmolive does fine. And he's got to smile with those white teeth . . . they're partly why we chose him."

Helen held her breath; the hair spray should be a good enough fixative, but with sweaty palms you never knew. Fergus straightened the tray on the sand so that it glittered more valuably, Sherif swept away footsteps in front with his palm frond, and Fergus lowered his hand for Philip to roll his camera. The blue draa draped itself beautifully as Daki, sitting on the ground, raised his forearms in delight, the blue ink showing handsomely on hands and face and arms, reached for the Zippy, picked it up beautifully with thumb and forefinger, and smiled a wondrous grin of sheer enchantment from ear to ear.

Except that he had no teeth.

Half an hour later Fergus, in blue from head to toe and his dark Welshness as Saharan as one could want, had turned over the cameras to Philip and Maurice and was trying to keep a straight face as he went through his own motions of commercial ecstasy over the soap box and brass tray. Three takes and it was pronounced perfect.

He threw back his head and roared with laughter. Rachid had explained, when the disgruntled Daki had been sent away, that he was not a true blue man at all, handsome though he was: he was a beach stud at Agadir, romancing anything and everything that paid, spoke five languages, had been given his dentures by a Swedish countess last fall, and had broken them this morning falling off his camel, which was undoubtedly the first one he'd ridden in his life.

"This is perfect, simply perfect," Fergus laughed. "Everything else in this whole impossible ridiculous project has been fake, it was too much to expect it wouldn't end up on that note as well."

"A farewell drink? Yeah. Let's stop the penny-pinching drinking in our bedrooms, and let Stanley be a big spender." Helen sat down at a table in the garden. "Glad you're finished, Fergus? I should think so. You're still very blue."

"Oh, yes, lady. So are you, by the way. I only wish there weren't that snake charmer to reshoot in Marrakech, though. Maybe he'll have decided that's a bit recherché too."

"I've had a bash, myself."

"Good. I had no idea you were so adept at forgery—you

saved our lives with the soap wrapper. You're full of unknown skills, aren't you?"

"Sometimes. I may have to borrow your plumbing, to
work on getting the ink off, the basin in my room's
stopped up. This ink seems somewhat indelible—are you
sure it isn't, Erica?"

"Of course not. We'll go to a hammam and steam it off
when we get home tomorrow. You both made great blue
men, I was quite gratified."

"Good. Suitably fierce on my camel? I was terrified."

"Suitably fierce." Erica smiled at her.

"Then it's worth it, although if I'm going to have to be
stained I'd rather have had henna . . . prettier." Philip
and Maurice came in from locking up the vans, fell into a
discussion with Fergus.

"What is it that kept Debbysue here so long anyway?"
Helen asked. "Not love of her beau after all, it seems. She
was rattling around quite happily without him; I had the
feeling she'd have been delighted if he'd stayed up in
Rabat where she thought he was."

"Oh, Helen, I don't really know. She was youngish
when she got here, and one of the few who really learn
the language, fit in, make friends among the country people. I think she hung around just to relax and have fun,
she'd worked hard for four years, don't forget. And then
what she's going back to just isn't as jolly as life here. It
does get to you, you know, having servants and life not
costing so much, the lovely countryside; she liked it all,
and it liked her."

"Good enough reasons for staying. I gather she *did*
work very hard?"

"Yes, she did indeed. The Center's not the same place
as when she took it over, or so I hear. I don't see how she
could stomach those boys, I never ever go there myself.
Horrid of me, I'm sure, but that's the way I am. But working hard here is a bit different from working very hard in

America or England. No maids to look after all the things they do here, cramped flats and buses and all. And the scrimping and shoestring bit; coffee-bar dates and second-run flicks, all that sort of thing. I've no intention of going back to that style myself, and I can see why she wouldn't be all that eager."

No, Helen thought, typing for an insurance company in Shreveport or whatever, it wouldn't be quite the same. More likely something in a hospital; she had all that experience at the Center, of course. But there *were* young doctors.

Fräulein, her head down like a charging bull and an unpleasant expression on her face, came marching down the garden from Stanley's old rooms, where Helen was ensconced, followed by a waiter with a wooden bucket full of tools. She stopped, seized the waiter's hand and held it out to Helen. "Your lavabo, Madame, the stoppage was caused by this, it is very very careless of you." Helen looked at the clot of bright yellow plastic, lumpy and moist. "You are leaving in the morning? Good. I will adjust your bill to encompass this negligence. There will, you may be sure, be a supplement."

"Lucky Erica to have nabbed a plane ride back with Jouti, they'll be there and soaking in hot martinis by now." Fergus shifted into fourth for what seemed the hundred and forty-seventh time, tooting the little horn that bleated not much louder than the roadside goat he was trying to avoid. "This car of yours hasn't any more pep than the bicycle you made us all go shares on for Sherif. Nice kid. Was he in ecstasy?"

"He was in ecstasy. Blissful. Unlike you. You could have gone with them too; you've the stomach for those little things with wings, I haven't." Helen began peeling a banana.

"No more does Digby, poor soul. He got into the most

elaborate web of falsehoods with Overton, trying to describe the view from the sightseeing plane, which he had eschewed out of terror."

"Didn't he go up either? Good man. If God had meant us to fly he'd have given us all credit cards. Good thing for Debbysue *she* didn't have any fears, though. I had the feeling Jouti would have stuffed her in a camel bag and sent her off to the airport that way, if necessary, to clear the decks for Erica. You don't like her, do you?"

"Dead right in one. She's damn good at her work, mind you, did twice what Gleb would have, but got paid twice the sum too. She's a professional, all right, whatever she does. Perhaps that's what I don't like. She had the room next to mine upstairs, you know. Middle of the night ultimatums outside on the balcony, laying it flat out that she'll deliver her fair white bod only when she's been given her own boutique in London. Bit whorish, really. Poor Overton."

"Poor Jouti, as well. She's pretty broke right now, I think, but still, if Stanley's backing her I would think he'd be a rock one could count on, I don't see him not delivering. If he promised her a boutique, a little payment in advance wouldn't hurt. A reneger he's not. When was this?"

"The night of Elfrieda, the shotgun—what a night that was, just as well to forget it."

"Yes, just as well to forget it."

CHAPTER X

"So that's that. I got bored with it all and just asked Jouti flat out what about my old friend Arthur? He said that was up to Stanley, and you say Stanley's havering and says it's up to Jouti. But they are both very enthusiastic about your work. That, however, you knew. The best hope I could find were the notes on that list of towns, with your initials . . . things Stanley meant to caution you about at that gorge; that speaks well. He'll probably drive you bats with things like that before it's all over, though."

Arthur nodded, shielding his eyes from the sun that beat down on the roof terrace of the Café de France. There was only a whisper of yellow in his eyeballs now, and his energy was returning enough for him to have thought of lunching here. "Vile food, but since I can't eat much anyway—" Ever the perfect host, Helen thought, struggling with a leathery omelet.

"Well, that's as you say. Still, I wonder if I should pursue it after all? Money's very tight just now, and will be. Overton Enterprise shares are all right, or I'd have unloaded mine, but perhaps I should think again. I wouldn't be surprised if they expected me to invest in these hotels. Ridiculous. Never ever put your money into your own work. I never have, never will. And there *is* that Arab at home that might be the better choice. When those chaps build, they build. Harems, for one thing—concubines, wives, slaves, mothers, eunuchs, garages, stables, helipads, the mind simply reels. I hear he has a personal fortune of thirteen billion—billion, not million—dollars. But at that, he's probably having trouble making ends meet. They do, you know. Dozens of everything from Rolls, Cartier, Dunhill. Poor man, he must feel hard-pressed every morning. So which to choose: an uncertain thing here that'll be a good thing if it does come off, or an impoverished dynast in a bedsheet?"

"Don't do either. Take a vacation instead. Enjoy." She waved her spoon at Djemma el Fna bustling below them, the fitful wail of flutes, Gnaoui drums throbbing, horns honking.

"We shall see. Can you possibly want that disgusting-looking crème caramel? Shouldn't you be watching your weight?"

"Yes, I do want it, and to hell with my weight. I need all the strength I can get—I volunteered to take Fergus to the airport at the crack of dawn tomorrow morning. I am compensating for the loss of his company ahead of time by overeating. I like that young man. And I'll miss him. *He* is good company."

They were early. The mountains were glittering in the just-rising sun and it would be a beautiful flight for Fergus. He had sent Philip and Maurice to return the rented vans yesterday; they would meet at the airport in Casa where Fergus was to change planes. Then London. She yawned, glad to see the coffee shop in the glass-and-tile atrium of the terminal was open, a waiter polishing the espresso machine. No one was at the newsstand yet, but she twirled the paperback book racks eagerly as Fergus checked his bags. All German, Dutch, Swedish, French. Ah, well.

"Sure you won't come on up with us? Dinner at the Savoy tonight?"

"Wretch," she smiled over a glass of orange juice. "No, I'd better hang in with Arthur a day or so more, those countesses show signs of wearing him out with their parties. But will you be at Crumbles for Christmas?"

"Christmas? I'd forgotten. In point of fact, I hope so, I'd planned to be. Have to see how editing this film goes, though. I'll be pale and wan from long hours in the darkroom, but you'll arrive bronzed, no doubt."

"If. We'll see. I'd planned to be there too, but so much has happened." A trickle of people were coming into the building now. The digital clock jumped relentlessly forward; a plane roared overhead, circled, landed. "Tell me a bit about Gleb; after all, you spent some time with him. Nobody seems to have known him very well."

"Gleb? Perhaps it's because there wasn't that much to know. Hard to say. Quiet, passive, did anything that came up that was necessary and not utterly disagreeable. He sat a lot. On little stools."

"Things happened to him, then, rather than because of him?"

"In a nutshell. He did speak excellent English, but I expect that was more his knack for languages than any great effort on his part, I don't know."

"That was something I wondered about; in his house, you see, there aren't many books, but they're all either in Arabic, which one would expect, or English. Nothing profound, thrillers, stories, westerns, so forth. But I'd have thought he'd have read German. Wouldn't that have been his second language after Latvian or whatever? Lots of German books all over town. Ooops, there's your flight being called." As they went toward the departure gate she said, "Just before he died—he hadn't the faintest idea who was there, just that someone was—I'm sure when I asked him what to do I said it in French—he was groaning and muttering something, I couldn't catch it exactly, but it was definitely in English, that I know."

She pushed her way through the crowd of travelers entering from the arriving flight and ran up to the observation terrace. How dear and fuzzy Fergus was as he strode across the field to the plane. Damn, she'd not replaced his socks. Oh, well. The thought of Christmas caused a pang of homesickness, not for home necessarily but for something, anything else but midnight muezzins, palm trees forever glittering and clattering, tangerines, lamb. She pulled off the tacky gold and purple scarf she'd bought in the souks and began waving to Fergus, who was climbing up the stairs to the plane.

"So it *is* you. I couldn't tell underneath that bit of gaud you were sporting."

"What?" She turned, seeing the plane begin to move out of the corner of her eye, and stopped breathing.

"I think I saw my looming offspring get on that plane? I'd hoped he'd be able to stay for a day or so, told him so in my cable. Ah, well, come along and help me find my bags, they're full of your playthings I thought you might want. Clothes, cameras, come along, come along."

Holding his hand tightly, she smiled. "Yes, Simon, I'm coming."

"You never told me his mother wore a great deal of black jet and very likely dined out too frequently?"

"Simon. In the first place I can't believe you've never met Arthur, and secondly that you could be jealous of anybody. And it was opals she wore; I remember her very well and she was quite a lovely lady. How is my varnish, by the way? Dry at last, I hope."

"Gone. As penance—I do hope my apologia arrived? Found the card in Portobello Road, very apt—I took up all the varnish, and a filthy job it was."

"Good. Serves you right. Your hands are like sandpaper, by the way. But all is forgiven, or almost all, and since I think things here are going to be for sale, there's a beautiful rug that would just fit—I'll show you—but I gather not just now, darling?"

"Not just now. What is your mattress made of, corn husks? Never mind, you're not. No, no carpet showing, not just now."

"No, Simon, you can't come in—two days here and the sun's gone to your head. Neva's here too and its ladies' day in the harem." Helen pulled the door to Erica's atelier closed behind her ruffled hair and half-off sweater, and Simon gladly moved down the gallery to the sunlit banquette and settled himself contentedly.

He could hear the whir of sewing machines farther along the gallery and, from the grilled window behind him, Helen's shriek of "Ninety-six?" assuaged by Erica's calm voice: "I know, it's devastating in centimeters, isn't it? Inseam—sixty-one—"

What frightful golf he'd played this afternoon, and how glad he was it was over. Not his game anyway, and he'd straggled along with Overton, Jouti, and Digby, a reluctant fourth, preferring to enjoy the walk and the weather when he should have been applying himself to manly competition. Games, games. He'd seldom seen the point of winning, preferring volleying for the joy of it rather than working at proper tennis, and the great fun of Scrabble wasn't the score, but discovering the new words one's opponent came up with.

A wasted afternoon, in a way. He'd made the mistake of asking Jouti whether the things in Kauder's house would be for sale—there was that carpet Helen wanted that he'd like to give her for Christmas. The trouble between Overton and Jouti had begun fuming then, at the third hole. It seemed Jouti had a mortgage, or whatever the equivalent in Islam was, on the house that Overton hadn't known about. No reason why he should—Jouti apparently owned a great deal of real estate all over the place, as well as olive and orange groves, cattle, and so on —but apparently he was intending to create a small, select hotel by connecting his restaurant, Dar Toubkal, to

Kauder's house, tearing down some enormous tenements between for gardens, a pool, adding another large house that he already owned next door.

Overton seemed to feel this was some sort of breach in their general scheme, which didn't include a hotel in Marrakech at all. Jouti, driving his ball with a vicious slice two hundred feet, had demurred; it was for his older sister, he explained, something of an annuity for her old age, she would never marry, certainly Stanley could understand these problems of family. His dear mother, she wished to keep the property in the medina in the family and it would soothe her last years to know he was trying to honor her wishes—alas, the only way to do so profitably was with this foolish little hotel, truly no more than an auberge, more the style of a private home, not a big operation at all. His younger sister's bridegroom was insisting on a dowry from the olive groves, it was all very difficult to be fair—

"Oh, I understand family property, *very* difficult to do the right thing by everyone." Stanley changed golf clubs, squinted at the green. "Takes the judgment of a Solomon sometimes. Bettman in on this?" He addressed himself to the ball at his feet, but his teeth were clamped down on his pipestem.

"Oh, it is very early for that, we have not decided about our own hotels yet, and after all, how could I have known before this—"

"Known you could get hold of the house so quickly? No way, I suppose, no way at all." He chipped, his ball fell into the sand trap alongside Jouti's. "Unless you had enough of a mortgage to foreclose any time you wanted to—oh, I know you can't practice usury here, but there are ways, I'm sure. Or unless, of course, you knew he was so ill he was going to die."

Erica must be talking with her mouth full of pins, Simon thought, as her voice floated out into the sunlight.

"Odd, isn't it, how chancy it is that any two people ever do meet—to think if your cousin hadn't died in Ifni you'd never have met Stanley."

"Isn't it? The afternoon he came to call—he'd brought Paul's things home from the prison camp with him, wallet, prayer book, a little silver cross, that sort of personal effect—I'd almost gone to the films; if I had I'd never have met him. He wasn't exactly the type then that Aunt Sarah would've encouraged to call again, I assure you. But he was heaven with her straight off, saw she was having none of Paul being dead, just went right on as if he'd be coming home any day. She'd even refused his pension or insurance or whatever they gave mothers. I'd had to go live with her when Mummy and Daddy died in the blitz, it'd been terrible to know what to do when Paul was officially declared dead—she simply wouldn't accept it, ignored it all."

"Then what effect did Stanley, who'd been there with him when he did die, have? The wallet and all?"

"She simply tucked them into a table drawer and said she was sure Paul would be glad to have them when he came home, and I was sent to the ·kitchen to make tea. Poor dear, she'd built her life around Paul since Uncle Graham died, and that was when Paul was two, I think. I wasn't even born then, and I hardly remember Paul at all, he was always away at school and older enough not to notice a little girl cousin, and then the war. But in any event, Stanley was wonderful with her, determined from the first to have me, you see—are you sure that's not going to be too long, I don't want to trip, you know—and she could be a gorgon, oh my word. Family, of course, but never a bean, Paul's father had been an inventor of sorts, but nothing much had ever come of it. She'd managed the right schools and so forth, but home was the most dreadful little flat, African violets and fading gentility."

"Could you turn to the left just a hair? Perfect—do go on."

"Well, Stanley got her drift right off; he was just beginning in advertising, slipped a snapshot of Paul from an album while Aunt Sarah wasn't looking, and returned it by post with a watercolor sketch he'd had one of the ad artists do from it, but of Paul in uniform and looking a bit older. Stars in his crown with Aunt, he had to be asked to tea to thank him."

"And so all walls crumbled? How very clever, and how sweet."

"Wasn't it? Shall I take it off now? Simply lovely, Erica, it's going to be a favorite, I can tell already. Yes, he was sweet to her; she wasn't really ga-ga, you know, just in that one area about Paul. Had been all his life, or at least *I* think so. He'd had diphtheria or something when he was a kiddy, and she'd promised God he'd be a priest if he lived—poor Paul, she kept him to it, I doubt he ever had a say in it at all or would have if he'd lived. Stanley understood that better than I ever could—he has a strong sense of justice himself—"

"Helen, if you like that try it on, but hike it up a bit at the waist, it'll be too long—patience, Neva, just this skirt to try now, you're heroic."

"Oh, I don't mind fittings—Stanley kept on the portrait thing for her all these years, from the time we were married; Paul in seminary, Paul ordained, and on and on . . . always a bit older, there are five or six of them around—I suppose I should give them to an art school? Well, it was just the ticket for her, of course; it wasn't long before she let him help her out with her 'affairs,' mostly Uncle's patents, and of course Stanley found just the one—the Wilcox process—something for dyeing synthetics nobody'd been able to pull off yet—you can imagine after the war, with nylon and all. He sold it in America, for dollars . . . she insisted he have his ten per cent commission, that was his first capital—"

"And the rest is history. Heavens, dollars in those days, she must have lived like a queen."

"Oh, no, stayed right on in the same horrid flat, waiting for Paul. But at least she was doing what she wanted to do, I think she had a happy fantasy."

"And now all that lovely lolly's yours. How nice. Just an inch off the pocket, I think, it's out of scale somewhere—"

"Eventually mine. She'd gotten some solicitor to draw up a will leaving everything to Paul, of course—poor man didn't know anything about it; there'll be a delay, but I'm the only family, so there won't be any other trouble. I must say it'll be nice to have a little of my own money, there's a tiny terrace I've always wanted to put in off my bedroom in Barbados—well, you still haven't told me what to wear to the do at the Center tonight, we're going on to something afterward, I think. Long or short?"

"Let's see—it's getting chilly again, maybe long. Helen, that looks wonderful on you, I'll have one of the girls leave that for you at Arthur's later, it just needs those two buttons moved a bit. Neva, why not let Stanley decide—he's always so interested in your clothes and how you look."

"I might as well; he always decides everything else, thank heaven."

The little basket from Sur Commande was in Helen's room when she and Simon came in from a long walk through the medina and an inspection of Djemma el Fna, busily at work in the cool twilight. The pigeon man was there, the Gnaoui dancers with their cowrie-shell hats and drums, the acrobats, basket sellers, storytellers. Simon had been intrigued by the medicine compounder squatting neatly with his tin boxes in tidy rectangles around him, a stack of clean green paper by his knees, the carefully crumpled cloth under which he slid coins and bills. An old woman had been squatting beside him, whispering symptoms into his ear; he flicked his small spoon from tin to tin, leaving round coins of colored powders on a paper, overlapping pale earth colors: green, rose, ocher, washy sienna, the turn of his wrist alone bespeaking assurance, prowess, and cure.

Coming in from the lingering warmth of the day, the bedroom was chill. She put on a sweater, heard Simon shuffling off to have a bath, the boom of the hot-water heater in the distance. Stanley was giving that Churchill painting to the Center tonight. Arthur insisted they all go and show the flag.

Almost at once that suspension, déjà vu, swirled over her like a gladiator's net; what was left of her mind that was her own told her to succumb to it, let it happen, it would be over sooner. Standing in the door of the Center, the little boy on the black-and-yellow cot with his braces on the bed beside him, the smell of cumin, a freshet of rain. The basket on her bed here, tied up in Erica's indigo and magenta floss, "I have it dyed just for me in Fès, my trademark," the sun on the rusty table in Ifni and the seams of Erica's jacket, Latif's body lying in the wet courtyard, the sheep hanging on its hook, a strand of the same floss caught in his broken glasses under the loom in the workroom. "I can't stomach those boys, I never ever go there myself. Horrid of me, I'm sure—"

"Lord, that runs with a reluctance, doesn't it?" Simon wandered back in, a towel around his neck. "Come look at that rug again while the tub fills, hmm?"

Helen shook herself free of bits of the gladiator's net, stood back while Simon pulled the rug into the light, absentmindedly agreed it was too handsome not to make a bid for. She sat down on a little stool, hearing Simon splashing at the end of the gallery. Arthur had left his boxes and bins out on the floor. That morning with Erica seemed a very, very long time ago.

She pulled the supple, heavy headdress out of the bin, scattering loose beads, broken fibulae on the floor; it fell like a heavily scaled felt snake across her hands. A last shaft of orange sunset lit the British identity disk set among the coins and coral, worn and scratched, but the Paul Wilcox quite legible.

The Vice Admiral sat in an armchair in the courtyard of the Garrison Center, his freckled, blue-veined hands clasped the arms like claws and his toes, in their cracked patent-leather pumps, pointed neatly in toward each other on the ground. All around him a babble of voices, many languages—but he did not notice, nor care that he did not notice. He had even forgotten that for years he had been put into his tartan trews, velvet jacket, decorations; dusted, brushed, transported here and there for this and that, what did it matter. Life was a long sleeping, more real in dreams these days than when awake, for in dreams his senses returned and he saw, smelt, heard, tasted. And understood, moved, bounded weightlessly across green meadows.

This clatter, this place—what—a painting, that fellow Overby or Underton, what did it matter. Winston had dabbled something one morning, so they said, that was it, now it was here. There was a gray-pink shimmering before his rheumy eyes, shot with iridescence now and again. Ladies in their gowns, too much French, he couldn't be troubled with it now. When he had taken the trouble he hadn't needed to, so many of his own countrymen in town, quite a good group, croquet, strawberries, English gardens or as close as anyone could manage in this place, and that was close enough, given a determined Englishwoman in a shade hat to keep the gardeners at it. All gone now, the pound worthless, those who were still alive were mostly in Spain now, drink was still cheap there, he was told.

"Your Excellency, may I present an admirer of yours, Helen Bullock, the photographer—" A brownish-beige blur in front of him this time. The woman had the perception to sit down so that her voice was at his ear level; he wouldn't have to keep his head up to hear.

"An honor, sir." A nice voice, American but low-pitched, good to hear his own language, and so many Englishwomen were screechers, no matter how much you admired their complexions. He couldn't listen to complexions.

"My pleasure, Miss—hope Winston's daub's been given a good spot; having a bit of trouble with my eyes just now."

"It looks very well indeed, so much charm in such a small thing."

His hands, which had been quivering with the effort of hearing, speaking, stilled on the arms of the chair, his lids sank, chin dropped. Helen sat on beside him, her own words echoing in her ears. So much charm in such a small thing; Neva was standing with Stanley, shaking hands with a group of latecomers.

The poor woman looks like a drowned Pekingese; the dull apricot velvet caftan was of a color that could only be carried off by someone with very swarthy or very white skin, not Neva's soft pink and rose; it dragged her silver-gilt hair into dust. Not only that, it was—off, somehow. It fit, of course, and yet it was too big, the sleeves too full for that small frame, the scale of the embroidery too heroic, the necklace of amber and silver, the earrings, dragged down the lines from her throat and showed Neva's neck as made of scrawny tendons, not as small, delicate, and graceful.

She did it on purpose, of course, Helen thought, sitting quietly. Happy Birthday dear Neva from Stanley via

Erica, your good friend. The bitch. Something else was wrong, aside from Neva's looking a good ten years older than she had this afternoon, and valiant in her awareness that the ensemble deliberately defeated her. What was it —dry, sallow, sere, the gold embroidery lighting long hard lines from her nose to her chin none had seen before, but that was not it, was it? The long lines, they were the same lines of pain Kauder had between those fierce bouts of pain, and the dusty sand of his beard was the color of Neva's hair.

"He sold off a company once—raking in the profits but not developing and expanding—" There was Digby, who had said that, bringing Neva a glass of champagne, SiOmar done up splendidly in shining white and crackling luminous glances at the ladies. The little pool had been planked over, covered with a rug, tubbed plants, and flowers; three musicians played society music there. Arthur came out of the atelier, which had been furnished with banquettes, rugs, a bar; he was sipping a Fanta and peering gloomily and crossly at a tray of spicy hors d'oeuvres that Kinza—resplendent in silver tissue and fresh henna—was passing. The "short boys" had been confined to the back quarters of the schoolrooms; none of these people would care to be reminded of them. Even the old Vice Admiral was being ignored; he no longer counted, he was a joke in his shabby little villa in the Hivernage to most of this world.

Two women, relentlessly British, paused on their way out, nodded at him dozing in his chair. "I must get over to him one day soon, those servants of his are robbing him blind, I see what they buy in the Marché, second rate cauliflower and I doubt he sees meat more than once a week, no wonder he looks so anemic. Great haunches of mutton for themselves, of course. Not only that—one expects a bit of thieving here and there—but they absolutely *abandoned* him at L'Aid this year. I went to call for him early that morning, before breakfast, he shouldn't be alone and not for a whole day—but they'd left the night before, can you imagine, he hadn't been able to get up to bed and was asleep on the living room couch."

"Nelly, that was good of you."

"Nonsense, he's one of us and it's no trouble. Oh, it's too sad, when I remember how lovely their place was when Dolly was alive and one could live on one's pension—"

Simon was in a corner full of Italian and Savile Row suits, there was a Very Important Personage indeed with Jouti and Stanley; whether they were talking hotels, or films with the Italian director, or trading rugs didn't matter, business was clearly being done. Probably because of the Personage, there was a newspaper photographer; Helen patted the Admiral's hand—"Cameras, sir, smile now"—straightened the faded tie and, as he raised his chin and opened his eyes, his lips puffing slightly, she slipped out of range as the flashbulb went off.

"Poor man's Dolce Vita, and on top of it Arthur's bound to overextend his capacities tonight, going off to that dinner. He'll moan and groan on his couch all day tomorrow, we'll be no good to him. Let's take a picnic out to the country?"

"And get our perspective back?" Simon took off his jacket and hung it in the armoire. "Yes, that'll be good. Where is it, by the way?"

"Where is what?"

"The postcard from Portobello Road I sent you—don't dissimulate. Neither of us can simply go to sleep and pretend it'll be gone in the morning."

"It's on the windowsill." Helen lay back on the bed, smoking. "What's the date on the back—oh, use *my* glasses, they're over there too."

Simon peered at the tiny line of printing dividing the

space for his limerick to her from the address. Bertrand, Blvd. Mohammed V, Marrakech, 1964, Imprimé en Maroc.

"Yes, well, there you are. Here we have the Koutoubia, the buildings the Center is now in here in the foreground —in black and white, I admit, but tatty ramshackle shutters where there are now a blue grilled window and kitchen door; cypress trees noticeably smaller. This is what he would have painted—equally beguilingly, I'm sure—in 'forty-three if he had painted what we saw tonight."

"He didn't."

"No, he couldn't have, certainly not in 'forty-three, and given it to very young Captain Overton. Stanley's stylish gesture for the Garrison Trust is an utter and absolute fake."

"Just like everything else, I'm beginning to think. Stanley's spurious largess *and* my handsome rings—one's real silver, but the other three with the little knobs and runes and doodads—they must be made of copper and melted-down hotel spoons, or something. Not silver at all, and I'm allergic to them."

Simon lay asleep in the thin winter sun, wrapped in a thick dark burnoose he had bought in the morning souk at Ait Ourir. Helen had almost forgotten he'd been in North Africa himself during the war, Tunisia, Libya; he was comfortable with the style of haggling in the weekly country markets. It'd been great fun, they'd bought tomatoes and oranges, had sandwiches put together from a loaf of hot flat bread stuffed with steaming roast lamb seasoned with cumin and the harsh pink salt of the countryside.

She threw the last crust at a stray goat who showed curiosity, lay back on the blanket listening to the sound of flutes, drums, clapping hands from some farm hidden in the valley below. High mountain meadow—in the spring there must be poppies, wildflowers here, and to come up from Marrakech in the summer it would be cool, wondrously fresh, especially along the banks of the little Ourika River that was glittering far below their perch.

Dear Simon—Debbysue and he would have liked each other, she thought suddenly, remembering the flashing humor of the transaction for the burnoose, the ease and simple humanness of him with the merchant, who insisted the stain was nothing, nothing, a little Tide, perhaps the tassel was a little old, but it had many more years in it, and the nubbly white djellaba the lady was examining, ah, that was new, *new*—the hole in the sleeve? Allah intended that, surely. Debbysue would have waded right in with them, she had none of Erica's disdain for less than perfection and probably would have found something for herself; if not, she would have enjoyed the process as much as the purchases, and after all that was really the point. Helen felt the next time she paid her income tax it might be with less of a pang; it had been a long time since she'd met such a good advertisement for the United States, and she hoped the Peace Corps had lots and lots of Debbysues. She must try to keep in touch with the kid one way or another, it'd be nice to see what happened to her next. Arthur was likely right, though: things would happen because of her, not to her.

Unlike Gleb. "He sat a lot. On little stools." Fergus, with his visual memory so like Helen's own. How clear it all was.

A Spanish prison camp in Ifni, Stanley and Paul Wilcox and Digby's father washed up on a rubber raft, tossed in among the other strays the Spaniards were keeping out of action for the Germans. Not the best of prisons, not the worst of prisons. Stanley, with his way to make in the world, undoubtedly organizing the facilities, the rations, very likely smart enough not to insist on distinctions be-

tween officers and enlisted men, he'd be one of the boys
and see that any other officers there were too, there
wouldn't have been many of either. Calisthenics, exercise,
games, lectures on whatever anyone knew about, French,
Spanish lessons, getting what medical attention and supplies were available for the wounded, the ill. He would
have been very busy indeed.

Paul would have been busy as well; Stanley would have
had him in charge of some sort of Morning Prayer, no
doubt, but more important, would have traded the boy's
talents to their captors for better food, for medicine—Paul
would have mended things, radios, cameras, watches, vehicles, he had all his father's talents. A useful prisoner to
have, Paul Wilcox, Blood Type A, C of E, on his identity
disks hanging around his neck with the cross on its chain
—the Spaniards would not have taken his cross or his
disks, those would have been King's X.

Who the Latvian had been, how he had come there
with the other Free French, I'll never know, Helen
thought, but his name had been Gleb Kauder and he had
died in that prison camp.

A large stork flew overhead, looking as if it had forgotten the diaper with the baby in it and left it on the greet-
ing card; it soared overhead, enormous, dipped toward its
large nest in the minaret of the village below.

Kauder had died in that camp, and Paul Wilcox had
chosen—for once had not "sat on a little stool," but had
chosen, perhaps, likely with Stanley's advice and help, certainly with Stanley's knowledge—to take on that identity
when they were released. No one would care, they were
only numbers to the Spanish in any event, Stanley had no
stake in the boy's life, and if he felt it'd solve the problem
of the gorgon mother back home, it was easily arranged,
he'd take some personal effects back, see that Paul's death
was verified, a piece of cake old boy, good luck—oh, keep

your identity disks if you want them, I'll say they were buried with you by mistake—cheerio.

Paul wandering out, Kauder's French papers, uniform, that would allow him to remain in the French Protectorate without undue problems, there was no need for him to speak better French than he did, since wasn't he, after all, a Latvian accident of war, how sensible of him to stay since "his country had Russians"—here was as good as anywhere else, then, so many windmills to repair, broken-down buses and trucks to work on, to drive, electric generators gone awry, he needed so little. A djellaba or two, shoes occasionally, the farmers liked his quiet manners in their villages, shared their little stools for him to sit on.

But he was not shy, as they were, in the city. He would go with them when they needed to sell an old rug, see they got better prices; he was among them, a friend, Si-Smaïl if the name Gleb was too difficult and strange—Smaïl, Paul's last joke against Sarah Wilcox. He survived, undoubtedly through his own lack of ambition and uninvolvement with any politics, the bloody turmoil of el Glaoui's deposition and death. The house was convenient and the taxes were low; by then he traded enough so the vanishing of the electric trains, golf carts, European clocks didn't matter.

Very likely it was only the accident of affluence that drew Stanley to Morocco on holiday that first time. Helen could see him energetically out one morning, Neva sleeping late or tanning by the pool, Stanley spotting a face, oh, of course—so he was still here, well, well, and how are things, any regrets? No, no, all well at home, your mother in the best of health, active in the Church, busy, I married your cousin, by the way, Neva Wilcox, she scarcely remembers you, of course she doesn't know either, a man has to make his own choices, no harm done to anyone, my card if I can ever do anything—yes, lovely country, bit of all right this sun in the winter. Marshall? Oh, a pity, he did die in the end, but made it home first, saw his family; left a baby son, I'm keeping an eye on them.

Not many meetings, over the years; what was the point, he was seldom in the city, preferring his friends far in the south. He was Smaïl, Ishmael, the desert exile, Sarah's sacrifice, the wanderer in wastelands that were his choice, not deserts to him at all. When a boy was born to a casual girl it was not of much import to anyone; perhaps it was just as well Allah then provided as he did. With the boy a cripple so very young, and his mother killed in the earthquake in Agadir, Latif had a home at the Center, was better off truly than he would have been as a street boy, a beach boy; he had crafts, education, could read and write, a home—Gleb, SiSmaïl, could, would have done none of that for him, sitting on little stools.

But then that eccentric woman's will—had he known of it, seen that copy of the Times that had been in his house? Had he cared? Likely not, Helen thought, either way. But Stanley could never have understood that, or been sure if he had understood that Paul truly was dead, that Gleb would never have resurrected him, probably scarcely remembered that life anymore, letting some handsome, hospitable village mother long long ago have an identity disk—what did he need them for after all, there was no more sentiment—for her daughter's headdress; had that daughter fallen on hard times, was the ornament here now to be sold? Who would ever know.

Not Stanley, to whom a fortune in money was a fortune in everything, worth the incredible efforts of thrashing about under cover of that convenient string of ridiculous television commercials trying to find Gleb, knowing enough to have circled on his road map all those meager spots around and south of Goulimine beginning in T. On the list in his file he'd done homework in London of the same sort, carrying the photograms to jog villagers',

farmers' memories with "Have you seen my friend?",
wanting the Polaroid of "Paul's" latest portrait to jog his
own memory—it was very true to what Gleb was now and
to what Paul would have grown into. A better forgery
than the "Churchill."

And why the painting at all? Whimsy, spur-of-the-
moment daredeviling because he had an artist on his
string painting fake "Paul Wilcox" portraits every few
years anyway? To endear himself even further to the gov-
ernment? Without cash under the table the hotels
wouldn't happen, of course, but this little bit of panache
wouldn't hurt. Not at all impossible for the hotel to dis-
cover an old footlocker, send it up to London to the man
who was a regular and important client now, for Stanley
to pretend he'd had the sketch cleaned, restored, and give
it back as a grand gesture? Churchill had only painted
one view of Marrakech in his life and that wouldn't be for
sale; the fake, hanging as it was on a dark tile wall now,
would be known of, but not often seen. Careless of Stanley to forget that buildings around the timeless Koutoubia changed even if the minaret didn't, but after last
night, who was likely to see or notice,

It must have seemed, in London, simple enough when
he thought Gleb was working on the film crew, could be
easily found. But if he didn't wish to be found—well, take
care of that son first, if Gleb didn't want the money for
himself he surely would for his own boy? Easy enough to
find a brown djellaba, he and Lalla Kinza were of a size;
nothing of him but hands and feet and calf of leg would
show, since he had brought several pairs of those sunglasses—a veil would cover his moustache, the rest of his
face. Henna on feet and hands from a Pentel, truss up his
trouser legs—the housekeeper favored djellabas with slits
almost to the knee, not wise to trust rolling them up alone
—with—what, no string of course, Stanley would not travel
thus—ah, there was that floss from the kimono basket

Neva had brought in from Erica's. The "short boys" were all going with SiOmar on the plane ride, nothing would keep them away from that, except Abdellatif, who had told him he had a chronic ear infection, could not go; no one would be at the Center for at least two hours, even that Bullock woman would go on the plane, of course—if she wanted to see the sheep slaughter she'd surely be curious to see the High Atlas from the air. Neva would sleep for the morning, as she did every few days now, calling it "instant face lift"; into his car then, the old Vice Admiral wouldn't know Fraterday from Thuesday anymore—park beyond the Hotel Chems, perhaps, change somewhere in that wasteland of pits and ruins and clumps of earth abandoned for once on this holy day by the derelicts who collapsed there, he would have a key of course, bustle busily past the hot-water man, in and out of the Center quickly. Abdellatif must have put up something of a struggle, though, in the atelier, his glasses hooked on a trailing bit of floss, smashed and kicked angrily under the loom, but still very quick; into the pool with the already dead boy and out again, throwing away the djellaba and scuffs in the wasteland, barefooting it back to the car in the sudden rainstorm. His suit had gotten soaked, he must have kept that veil to wipe the Pentel off his hands and the mud off his feet before putting on his own shoes and socks, balled it up and shoved it under the seat with the windshield cloth. Neva still sleeping, his suit would have had to "fall into the tub": there was no way it could have gotten so wet just having driven to the Hivernage and back.

One less heir. But still, no Gleb in Taroudannt. South, then—was it Tiznit? Tafraoute? Tan-Tan? Tagannt? Tabahnift? Tigouraine? Small places, Erica had said, so many of them. Very well, the gods had given him the film crew for perfect cover, all so godforsaken down here he'd have to keep them busy, busy—ramparts, then, build ramparts, not exactly out of keeping with his flair—he would have decreed pyramids if necessary, Helen thought.

And all the while Gleb was ill in Goulimine . . . he must have heard "Overton" from Fergus up in Taroudannt, as bothersome as a buzzing fly, and, as he must have done many times over the years, simply left, to avoid bothersome meetings, reminders of an almost forgotten past. He must have thought Digby and I were in Tiznit just for the day, going back up to Taroudannt where the film was to have been finished, and if he kept on going south, he'd be left alone. But he'd gotten only to Goulimine before another sudden seizure with his old enemy, hepatitis; unable to move, but safe enough, good old Elfrieda would look after him, all he could do was lie in bed in any event in the acute stage; he must have heard all our voices, Stanley's after he arrived, but there was nothing to do, no reason anyone should know who was in number 8.

Had he ever known, or had the Nembutal which Stanley, thinking to dissolve their telltale gelatin in his washbasin, must have tipped from many yellow capsules into— a twist of paper?—and dropped in the tiny teapot the night of the shotgun, put him so sound asleep—on top of Fräulein's laudanum—that he hadn't known when Stanley had come in, poured most of a bottle of brandy down his throat?

The old French joke, "*L'alcool tue lentement*," and its response, "*Bien, je ne suis pas pressé*"—but it had killed Gleb quickly enough, and hideously. He must have known something, those last hoarse words of his in English: "Why, Captain, why why why?"

She pulled a spear of grass with a tasseled head from the ground, tickled Simon's neck. "Wake up, Simon, I have to tell you things—"

It was cold; the sun had left the meadow around them to send out damp rich odors by the time she'd finished talking. He took her hand.

"Why?"

"The money, it must be, some quirk in Stanley must make him feel it would be very unfair for Neva not to have it; it was only because of Stanley, after all, that there *was* any money. Paul would never have done anything about his father's patents even if he'd come home. I can imagine him 'sitting a lot on little stools' too, in seminaries, or laboratories if he'd gotten away from Mum, but not hustling about selling patents he wouldn't have known about. Stanley created that fortune, and in his head it was only right it should go to Neva; she'd had the care of old Aunt Sarah for decades, perhaps it'd been tiresome. Fair, right, and just. I think he must have assumed automatically without thinking about it that Paul, or Gleb, whatever, would have come forward—nothing in his life fits that, he could have made a lot of money here, lots of people have; he only wanted enough to live simply on, and he had that."

"Nothing to be done about it, you know." He looked at her quizzically.

"I know. Abdellatif—that was never questioned as anything other than a very likely accident, and Stanley himself spiked all guns by saying straightaway he gave Gleb the brandy. Nothing to be done. Neva might as well have her million, whether she wants it or not. I rather think she'll want it a great deal more than she thinks she does now, though."

"It's as I've always said, the best belly dancers in the world are Jewish girls from the Bronx. This one doesn't need dancing lessons, she needs thyroid pills. Lazy isn't in it." Arthur was pushing his way through an audience in double-knit suits and drip-dry evening dresses. He had identified them as being radiologists from Teaneck, New Jersey, and was consequently oblivious of the *pssts* and *h*sses protesting his interruptive exit. The dancer had barely begun, but Helen privately agreed she'd not get better, only finished.

She followed Simon and Arthur beyond the restaurant and into the Casino, a glacial carpeted room with an expanse of empty tables, light that seemed to come from brown bulbs, if such things existed, and one croupier dealing twenty-one. She peered through large glass doors; more tables, roulette, baccarat, but dark, closed, empty.

"This may very well be worse than the dancer—garçon!" But no waiter appeared for Arthur. Helen had a raging thirst from the rich dinner of flaky bstella, stuffed pigeons, and sweet couscous with cinnamon they had been served; she desperately wanted beer.

"Hallo, hallo." Stanley left his chips on the table, turned around and came over to them. "Dismal, isn't it? Trouble is they don't let the restaurant crowd know there's gambling in here—they all topple back into their buses after the floor show and totter off to bed. Beat money off with a stick, the management. Let's get some drinks organized, Neva'll be back in a second, she'll want a hand or two. Having a good holiday, Father Bede?"

"Exceptional. But I'm afraid, since it was very spur of the moment, I must be leaving."

"Pity. I hope you're not going to take Helen with you?"

"That's up to her, of course, but I rather hope so. Arthur seems to have recuperated at a tremendous pace."

"I may look so, but it doesn't do to be reckless. Helen, shall I paint myself yellow to keep you here?"

"No. I'd not believe it, I've been through quite enough of that sort of thing. You're fit as a flea, and I want to watch Fergus edit some of his film; if I don't get back to London soon he'll be finished, the rate he works."

"Film?" Overton, who looked feverish, glittery, she

thought, wiped his brow. "Oh, yes, yes, the soap things—very talented and delightful son you have, Bede. Give him my best, hope we'll work together again one day."

"And you, Arthur, are you and Stanley going to work together on the villa and—" Helen drained her glass of beer.

"We're in the middle of negotiations with a builder, he's asking enough to build a duplicate of the Koutoubia just now, but that'll change. If they begin in January I'll need to be here in March. Otherwise, I think not?"

Stanley seemed not to have heard the challenge, summoned the waiter again.

"You think not. So, Christmas?" No point asking Arthur to Crumbles, he'd detest every inch of it.

"I'm taking Erica to Rome with me in case I have a relapse. Besides, it's time that girl gets out into the world, I want to jog her to live up to her talents. She's just pried loose some money a London shop's been owing her—time to clear up the loose ends here at last. Tide which when taken at its flood, all that. Very demure about it, but there's a silent partner waiting in the wings to get her off to a start in London. She's promised me a tiny piece of the action. So difficult to find any good investments these days, it quite takes away the point of my making more money, but I'm sure Erica's going to turn out to be blue chip." He rose, pulled out a chair for Neva. "That might do for the name of her boutique—Blue Chip."

"But then you're all leaving, so I hear? How dreary. But the Farringtons are here, Stanley darling, and those nice Italians whose name I never can remember. If you're sending Digby up to London day after tomorrow he'd better bring down some clothes for me, I think it's going to be rather gala. Do take some aspirin, here—" She pulled a pillbox from her little bag. "He has a terrible headache, but you know men, they refuse to admit they're ever ill."

Epilogue CRUMBLES AGAIN

Digby Marshall adjusted the reading lamp in his sitting room to his liking and reached for a typescript on the table beside him. He'd had to perfect his typing quickly when Overton had tapped him as personal secretary; as an exercise he'd set himself the task of transcribing his father's wartime diary. The faded holograph on shabby paper was bound to be more difficult that anything Overton would likely ever give him.

He'd read it before, several times, as a boy and as a young man; Dad had seemed a nice chap as far as one could tell from notes jotted in prison camp. Such conditions would bring out the essential in one, perhaps; Dad had been ill the entire time, too.

It was shivery in London; he flicked on his electric fire. But it was pleasant being sent back for a week, he could have some time entirely to himself, for one thing.

"—the Capt. says Paul, he, I the only ones from plane. Paul swam with me on his back to raft or I would have bought it. We are in Spanish camp he says, Ifni? Awful hole, no doctor my leg's bad and head too, but some here worse off so doesn't do complaining. Paul never stops nursing us, Captain trying organize some medicine from Spaniards—"

The months of lying in weak survival, Paul finding a way to raise the beds of the ill so they could see out the one window, rigging cloth fans from the ceiling so they could, with a string, fan away the flies themselves— "My kid must be born now, I wonder if Annie knows I'm alive—"

"—not long now, Paul got a bit of a listen to a radio he was fixing for a guard, Germans about finished. So are we. Chap next to me died this morning, Latvian he was, only talked a bit of German and French, don't know whose gangrene stunk worse, his or mine, but—"

"Hi there, Digby, Merry Christmas ahead of time." Helen Bullock stood in his doorway.

"Why, why—hello, Helen. Goodness, I hadn't expected—"

"I know. That 'shipboard' feeling, seeing each other out of context. You look great. Listen, I came to see if you had an inkling of where old Fergus has holed himself up? He's not at his office or his flat."

"Oh, I'm afraid I don't—I can get onto Mr. Wranklin at Aurora tomorrow, if you like. The soap's their account, they would know, I'd think."

"Would you? That'd be wonderful. No, no brandy, thanks. I'll call you before noon—Simon and I are off to the country at last, we've been doing some errands and things in town, but I hope he's finished now. Talk of déjà vu—Simon's little hideaway's on Church Street—I was on King's Road and see Braid Trade's having a 'going out of business' sale, and the shops on either side too. Could I be right in supposing there'll be a new modiste there under the aegis of Overton Enterprises and Arthur Bettman, Inc.?"

"Um, um, Mr. Bettman is, of course, free to—I really can't—"

"Of course, forget I asked. How's all the hassle with Neva's inheritance, getting cleared up swiftly, I hope?"

"I believe so, I'm taking some papers from the lawyers back to Marrakech when I go. All very routine."

"It would be. All very routine. Now."

"Helen—as long as you're here, could—would you read this?"

Half an hour later Digby finished his brandy, stood up and sat down for the fourteenth time. "This Paul Wilcox seems to have been such a decent sort, you see—not just saving Dad's life, but all those other things in the camp for everyone—didn't he more than earn his right to live as he wanted for as long as he chose? I don't think he was allowed that last choice."

"No, he wasn't allowed that last choice. But there's nothing we can do about it, don't you see. Nothing."

"There's nothing I can do about it, then, is there?"

"No, Neva, there's nothing—there never was, from the beginning. You mustn't think that. This, well, this is something I must do, that's all. Call it what you like, foolish fifties, May-December, she's—she's a new beginning for me. A child, I hope, as well."

"Yes, I quite see that. I was always sorry I—" Neva looked out the window at the Mamounia gardens, the orange trees bearing blossom and fruit at the same time. "Then you'll be leaving tomorrow? You aren't well, Stanley, you've had that fever for days, and you're coughing now, you shouldn't travel."

"It's nothing. Yes, I'll be in Rome for Christmas, we can begin to arrange things when you come home after New Year's."

"I shan't be coming home. One of your men can come out to Barbados to 'arrange things' if you like. I'll want that for myself, and I shall be expensive, Stanley—even with Aunt Sarah's money I shall be very, very expensive."

"There's nothing you can do about it, Erica, you're in Rome now. You'll have to put up with being whistled at and pinched and ogled, so enjoy it." Arthur summoned a waiter, ordered Erica a Negroni and a tonic for himself.

"I may be in Rome, but I'm glad I shan't be here long. I've had enough of that in Morocco to last a lifetime."

"What about that villa Stanley's building you back in Marrakech? Now, now, no blue-eyed surprise, Bo Peep— when he began specifying seven-foot tubs in milady's bath, clothes poles eight inches higher than Neva could ever use even to hang herself from in despair, a vanity with the washbasin forty inches high, could I not envisage a somewhat tall woman? No, no, I was silent as the grave—but tell me, what color bathroom fixtures, as long as you have a choice; he rather thought one of the Italian floral porcelains?"

"None. I've no intention of having anything to do with any of it, no matter what his fantasies are. I'm finished with Morocco. The troops are paid off, the Hadj has the house key, I've sold the machines, turned in my residence card, and I am out, finished."

"How efficient, how enterprising. Then all's signed, sealed, and so forth for London? You do know I wish to invest modestly?"

"I do, and you may. He's joining us here after breaking the news to Neva, tomorrow or the next day, I forget—I suppose I should go meet his plane. Yes, there's to be a lease in my Christmas stocking, curled in with a judicious number of shares in his Enterprises. Deed to a little flat. All those nice Christmas stocking stuffers—" she smiled.

"And what will there be in his stocking? A bit more than a well-turned ankle, one hopes—hasn't he served his seven years, so to speak, by now?"

"Perhaps. But in his stocking? Nothing."

"Nothing? My dear Erica. Audacious! Even I had thought—"

"You all thought what you liked—no one seems to have consulted me. As you yourself say, I'm by way of being a blue-chip investment, and other than that, I've paid my dues. I bought Stanley a brown djellaba in the old clothes souk for *his* Christmas present. A lady's djellaba."

"What does that have to do with anything—you don't mean he's a secret drag queen, I hope?"

"Don't be foolish. Actually, I'm not quite sure myself exactly what it means, but I'd rather not know more; this is just enough so I can do as I please, and I do *not* please to be the second Lady Overton or any version thereof. Something better, when I'm about sixty-seven, seventy, I should think. Much better."

"What?"

"Dame Erica. Dame Erica Portland, and all on my own."

"Nothing to be done?" Erica looked up from the newspaper on her lap at the doctor who had come out of Stanley's hospital room. Arthur had gone off in search of a drink of water, pointing out the story in the paper about yet one more clash between oligarchy and monarchy in Morocco, which had left Jouti among several other Ministers without portfolios and very much in retirement. "Just as well I hadn't counted on those hotels, that won't get off the ground for years now."

The doctor sat down across from her. "No, he is not uncomfortable so much, but until his own doctors arrive I think it better we do no more. He is in no danger now, but the paralysis is deeply developed, deeply."

"I didn't know anyone but children got this—in this day and age, with the vaccine—*polio*, for heaven's sake."

"Oh, yes, adults as well. He had somehow missed having the vaccine, his generation I suppose, most unfortunate. At his age I think he will make some slow recovery, but very very slow, surely always a wheelchair, perhaps with therapy, braces, but that is much in the future. It is ironic, no, he must in truth have contracted this at one of the centers he is so generous with. Now, if you wish to see him?"

"No. No, I don't. His secretary will be here from London tomorrow, with the doctors, they'll take care of it all. No point my seeing him, there's nothing I can do."

"Nothing more to be done, Simon, we tried everywhere and he's just gone to earth. I do the same thing myself when I have a deadline. He'll be along when he can. Ohh, look, the Baggie's gone!"

Not only was Mr. Penner's plastic sheeting gone from the roof, but the new thatch was in place, the mud was covered with a quilt of snow, and the kitchen had been thoroughly cleaned—the linoleum waxed, the windows washed, and a fire laid in the grate.

"Simon, how cozy—did you scrub your fingers to the bone?" Helen put down suitcases, baskets, looked about with pleasure.

"No, I do claim credit for getting the varnish off, but this—" Quizzically, he flipped lights on in the dining room, the hall; Helen shoved luggage down the bare hall floor to Simon's large warm bedroom, finding it all fresh and attractive, the horrible depressing phase of work and sheer hanging-in well worth it after all.

"Helen!" he roared from the living room. He was standing in the doorway, beyond him against the deep bay window was a bushy, fresh, aromatic Christmas tree, trays of ornaments around it on the floor.

"Oh, of course, then, Simon, he's here—silly of us not to have thought of it. Peace and quiet, no telephone. Let's hope he's finished and that we're not intruding. If he had time to clean the kitchen the thing must be done."

Simon was lighting the fire in the broad, low hearth when lights of a car raked the beamed ceiling, doors slammed, and voices came up the path. They heard the stamping of feet, the crackle of groceries being put down in the kitchen.

"Hey there, Fergus," Helen called from her chair by the living room fire, "remind us always to ask the agency for you. That's quite a job you did in the kitchen."

"Not I." He smiled contentedly from the doorway. "Much too busy, but I'm finished at last."

"And thank heavens you are—maybe now you can help me turn over that old mattress on your bed. I'd like to box it up and send it down to old Fräulein Elfrieda, it's just her style. Hi there, Helen. You must be Fergus's daddy, it's a big pleasure to meet you, sir. I'm Debbysue Kemp."

"Well, you see the flight I was on had to make this little stop in Tanger, see, and I thought, well, I hadn't visited Nouzha and Hamid for a long time, so I kind of took a stopover. My, it was nice, I got the most gorgeous sugar hammer I've ever seen, and then when I got back to the airport a few days—well, not *quite* a week—later, there was Fergus with Philip and Maurice having a drink while their flight picked up passengers for London. And somehow I thought, gee, I hadn't been in London since I was eighteen, and then I had to spend all my time being polite and proper in the embassy and that wasn't any fun at all—so—"

"Oh. Oh, good God, *that* Kemp."

"Well, yes, Helen, *that* Kemp. You remember, Daddy went into a real tailspin when Mama died, but now he's tired of being retired and sitting around in Shreveport, so he made a big contribution to the party and has a nice new appointment—I don't know where it is, but it'll be another embassy and there's only me, I'll be running his house and all that, stuck for years I'll bet. I'm glad I'm having some fun while I can—I don't have to be home till after New Year's. One good thing, I did get Morocco out of my blood at last."

"Well, dear, yes and no. Where—" Helen reached down to the floor, rummaged in her capacious bag, pulled out a *Times*. "Oh, now this is apt . . . can you do English crosswords, Deb? Blind rodent after artist. 5."

"No, I can't."

"Well, it's Rabat. Which is exactly where you're going to be keeping house—or embassy—for your daddy. Says right here on the front page he's just been appointed our new ambassador to Morocco."